SAVING THE BEST FOR LAST

"Where are we going?" April Thorgard asked as they rode their mounts side by side through the night.

"I said I'd find a night and a place," Skye Fargo told her as they reached the clearing he had selected that afternoon.

He dismounted first, then lifted her to the ground. Her lips reached up to his and he let his hands roam along the softness of her voluptuous body. Then she stepped back, unbuttoned her shirt and let it fall from her shoulders. She yanked her skirt free, pushed down and then stepped out of her bloomers. For an endless moment she stood naked before him in the moonlight.

"Make me forget all the horror, Fargo," she said, moving into his arms. "Just for a while."

"That's what I'm aiming to do," said Skye, as he set out to make this a night to remember—even though it might be their last alive. . . .

THUNDERHAWK

by
Jon Sharpe

A SIGNET BOOK
NEW AMERICAN LIBRARY

PUBLISHER'S NOTE

SIGNET TRADEMARK REG. U.S. PAT. OFF. AND FOREIGN COUNTRIES
REGISTERED TRADEMARK—MARCA REGISTRADA
HECHO EN CHICAGO, U.S.A.

SIGNET, SIGNET CLASSIC, MENTOR, ONYX, PLUME, MERIDIAN and NAL BOOKS are published by New American Library, 1633 Broadway, New York, New York 10019

First Printing, November, 1986

1 2 3 4 5 6 7 8 9

PRINTED IN THE UNITED STATES OF AMERICA

The Trailsman

Beginnings . . . they bend the tree and they mark the man. Skye Fargo was born when he was eighteen. Terror was his midwife, vengeance his first cry. Killing spawned Skye Fargo, ruthless, cold-blooded murder. Out of the acrid smoke of gunpowder still hanging in the air, he rose, cried out a promise never forgotten.

The Trailsman, they began to call him all across the West: searcher, scout, hunter, the man who could see where others only looked, his skills for hire but not his soul, the man who lived each day to the fullest, yet trailed each tomorrow. Skye Fargo, the Trailsman, the seeker who could take the wildness of a land and the wanting of a woman and make them his own.

Wyoming, 1860, an untamed land where
the good and evil in men's souls
come together as surely as
the waters of the Wind River and
the Bighorn meet . . .

1

On a warm summer afternoon it began.

That was the start of it. And the end, too, most everyone said.

But they were wrong.

It began as silent and fierce as the red-tailed hawk's dive, with a strike so swift its prey hardly has time to cry out. On a warm summer afternoon, just south of the Bighorn Mountains, five wagons rolled northward. Four were big Conestogas with reinforced hickory axles and one an Owensboro seed-bed wagon carrying extra water casks, tools, and supplies. The wagon train had started in Utah, its destination the rich farming land of Montana Territory. It was perhaps one of the grim twists of fate that it was not a larger, stronger wagon train, but three wagons had never arrived to join. Yet Hiram Dodd, the wagonmaster, decided to go on, anyway. Dreams are impatient travelers.

Like all those who braved the untamed, uncharted land, each had come for his own reasons. Each carried his own baggage of hope, the wagon train a symbol of a new life. But to the near-naked, bronze-skinned horsemen unseen in the thickness of the box elder, the wagon train was another kind of symbol. It was the mark of the intruder, of those who came to rule, to command, to own the land when the land was no one's to own. Worst of all, they cloaked themselves in fine words but left a trail of broken promises. Like the weeds that threatened to choke a pond, they had to be cut down.

The tall warrior with the intense, black-coal eyes wore a hawk's beak pendant around his neck. When he raised his arm and brought it down in a short, chopping motion, the cry of the Cheyenne sounded in the warm, summer afternoon. Their attack was as perfectly executed as it was fierce. They came in waves of galloping ponies, each wave firing arrows in alternate volleys. In seconds, the blue sky was almost invisible through the flying shafts that seemed to go on endlessly.

The wagons were never able to form a circle, unable to halt and unable to flee. The attack was merciful only because it was over so quickly. On a warm, summer afternoon—an attack on a wagon train, like so many that had come before and after.

But that was five years back.

Since then, there had been five years of warm summer afternoons. That particular afternoon was but a footnote in the history of broken dreams.

And now it had been born again.

Not that the big man with the lake-blue eyes knew it, not yet. All he knew was a sense of disbelief that was fast spiraling into anger inside him, and he peered hard at the man that faced him from the other side of the old desk. "You're damn right I don't understand it, Will Conklin," Skye Fargo said. "You send for me to ride trail for you and now you say you can't take me on?"

The rancher's normally relaxed face struggled uncomfortably and his fingers nervously turned a key chain. "I'll pay you for your traveling time here, Fargo," he said. "I can't do more'n that."

"Hell, Will, you know I don't care about that," Fargo snapped. "I can go to Jack Tisdale. He's always wanted me to break trail for him."

"He won't take you on, either," the rancher said. "Not now."

Fargo felt the frown digging deeper into his brow. "What the hell is this all about, Will?" he rasped.

"It's about Bertram Thorgard. He wants to see you and he got the word to us," the rancher said, his lips pulling back in distaste.

"Who the hell's Bertram Thorgard?" Fargo blurted.

"Bertram Thorgard is a lot of money and a lot of power," Will Conklin said.

"He own you? Jack Tisdale, too?" Fargo demanded.

"No, but he owns the bank, and the bank holds notes from every rancher around here. That includes me and Jack. Word came down that we hire you and the bank calls in our notes," the rancher said.

"Son of a bitch," Fargo grunted.

"Just what I said," Will agreed. "But I can't have my notes called up now. Neither can Jack or any of the others. I don't know the man, never met him, and he's got my hands tied."

"Why the hell didn't he just send word for me to come see him?" Fargo asked himself as much as Will Conklin.

"Bertram Thorgard does things his own way, I hear," the rancher said.

Fargo's eyes flared blue ice. "I don't much like his way," he growled.

"Don't blame you, old friend. But he does want you. I'd pay the man a visit," Will said. "His place is north of Shadyville up past the Sweetwater."

Fargo let himself frown into space for a moment as his thoughts leapfrogged. "Only two reasons I'll pay him a visit," he growled finally. "One, Vivian Keeler's got a place in Shadyville and I've been promising to visit her for two years, and two, to tell Mr. Bertram Thorgard it's not smart to try to lean on me."

"I imagine you'll do that real well," Will Conklin said, coming around the desk to put his hand on the big man's shoulder. "I'm sorry, I didn't want to go along with this. I just couldn't help it."

Fargo's chiseled face relaxed, and a smile came to his lips. "I understand, Will. Pay off that note and be a free man again," he said.

"Quick as I can, that's for sure," the rancher said, and with a handshake, Fargo strode out of the house to where his horse waited beside the hitching post. The magnificent Ovaro seemed to shine in the afternoon sun, the jet-black fore and hind quarters gleaming, the midsection pure white. Fargo swung into the saddle and turned the horse northward across Wyoming Territory. He rode hard, the anger still inside him. The colossal nerve of Bertram Thorgard defied belief. He was plainly an arrogant man with the power of his money and willing to use that power any way he could. Men such as Bertram Thorgard came to believe the world and everyone in it was made for them. He would have to be told differently, Fargo grunted as he crested a long hill and started down the other side.

His eyes scanned the land as he rode, the habit as much a part of him as his skin. This was redman's land. The Arapaho rode here, and sometimes the Assiniboin ventured down from the north, as did the Sioux. But mostly this was Cheyenne land and it was easy to understand why the Indian fought so savagely for this countryside. Wyoming Territory provided both forest and plains and every kind of game for every kind of need: buffalo and antelope, deer and jackrabbit on the plains; moose, elk, bear in the forests; game for food and hides, for furs and robes, and plenty of badger, otter, and beaver for small pelts. But for all its richness, it was a fierce land where winters came on killing winds. Yet the land provided for those who knew how to meet it on its own terms.

It was a land where trial and hardship could bring out the best in men's souls. And where the opportunities for unbridled greed and power could bring out the worst, Fargo added grimly, and he immediately thought of Bertram Thorgard. But he pushed the man's name aside and let his mind turn to more pleasant things as he rode alongside a deep stand of dark-green balsam. Vivian would be well worth the trip. He smiled and memories rushed at him—remembrances of warm, eager lips, of clasping legs that were smooth tentacles of desire. But mostly he remembered a woman wise enough to understand her own needs and strong enough to abide by them. Vivian had married because her husband needed a woman to do a woman's work and she needed a provider. There had been an understanding—an arrangement—and loving was never part of it. When he died, she'd carried on to find a new life for herself at another time, with other needs.

In between, Fargo smiled again, he'd met her and it had been good, real good. Vivian was a woman you could respect out of bed as much as you could enjoy her in bed, and that wasn't easy to find. The smile still edged his lips as he saw the long shadows marching down the rolling hillsides. A salesman with a glass-windowed delivery wagon hung with pots and pans came into view along a road, and Fargo sent the Ovaro across his path.

"The Sweetwater's dead ahead of you, mister," the man said in answer to Skye's question. "And Shadyville's straight on."

"The Thorgard place?" Fargo asked.

"You can get there without going through Shadyville," the man said. "Take a left soon as you cross the Sweetwater. Follow a thin line of yellow poplar. It'll lead you right to his spread."

Fargo nodded thanks and sent the pinto into a canter until he came to the narrow river, found a sandbar that afforded easy crossing, and rode to the other bank. He spotted the long, thin line of trees at once and followed their path to reach a large ranch as dusk began to settle across the land. He rode past neat, well-kept post-hole fencing to arrive at a large house, the bottom fieldstone, the top good oak shingle, with two chimneys and a gabled window at one side of the roof. A rich man's house, he decided as he halted at the front door, dismounted, and left the Ovaro at a brass-topped hitching rail. Two large stables took shape behind the main house and he glimpsed ranchhands at their chores. The front door of the house opened as he reached it, and he faced the man, whose bulk loomed large in the doorway.

"You're Fargo," the man said in a voice that resonated with authority. He was a big man with a heavy face, hair still black though the man looked to be in his fifties. His face had disdain in its every line—the jutting jaw, the cold blue eyes, the wide mouth that turned down at the corners.

"Good guess," Fargo said.

"No guess. I was given a good description of you. I'm Bertram Thorgard," the man said.

"I know," Fargo said.

The man's thick brows arched. "You were given a description of me?" he ventured.

"Let's say you fit what I expected," Fargo said.

"What's that?" Bertram Thorgard asked.

"Somebody who needs trimming down to size," Fargo snapped.

The man's smile was one of tolerant amusement. "I expected a certain amount of resentment," he said smoothly.

"You got it," Fargo growled.

"Please come inside," the man said, and Fargo followed him into a huge living room furnished with heavy, mahogany furniture, rich maroon drapes framing the windows, and tapestries on the walls. It was a quietly opulent room that fitted Bertram Thorgard comfortably.

"You've a brass pot full of nerve, Thorgard. What makes you think you can maneuver folks around to suit yourself?" Fargo frowned.

"You're here, aren't you?" Thorgard said diffidently.

Fargo felt himself flare at the smug truth in the man's answer. "For my own reasons, not yours," he flung back.

"Reasons don't interest me. Results do," Bertram Thorgard said.

The man was not easily ruffled, Fargo conceded inwardly. "Why didn't you send word to me you wanted to talk? Why all this beating around the bush?" Fargo threw at the man's calm disdain.

"I was ready for you when I heard Conklin had sent for you. I wanted you now, not later, after you'd finished with him. Besides, I wanted you to have reason to listen to me," Thorgard answered. "You must at least be curious."

"Talk fast. I don't listen long," Fargo said, ignoring the question and the truth it contained.

"I've two thousand dollars for you, Fargo. That is a lot of money," Thorgard said.

Fargo felt his brows arch. "A powerful lot of money," he agreed.

"I'm going to bring my grandson back to me. I need you for that," the man said, his heavy face darkening suddenly and an urgency coming into his voice.

"Why?" Fargo asked, his eyes narrowing.

"To find him, first. Then to take him," the man said. "The Cheyenne have him."

"They take him in a wagon-train attack?" Fargo asked.

"Yes, and now I'm ready to take him back," Thorgard said.

"Just like that. Just walk in and take him back," Fargo remarked, sarcasm thick in his voice.

"No, not just like that. I know how hard it will be," Thorgard said, and leaned forward, his heavy face growing more massive. "But I've planned out every part of it. For three years I've prepared, and now I've put it all into action. I've used all the power of connections and money. I've picked my men, arranged details, laid out plans for escape and pursuit. I can't fail. All I need is you, the Trailsman, the very best, to find that red devil that has my grandson."

"There are a hell of a lot of Cheyenne," Fargo said.

"I know that. That's why I need you, to find the right one," Thorgard said.

"How old is the boy?" Fargo asked.

"Six," the man said.

"It'll be like looking for a needle in a haystack. Lots of kids are taken in wagon-train attacks," Fargo said.

"There are things to help you. His mother was taken in the attack, a very blond young woman, and I know exactly when and where the attack took place," Thorgard said.

"How do you know that?" Fargo queried.

"A man who reached the scene an hour after the attack," Thorgard said.

Fargo fastened Thorgard with a probing stare. "Even if I could find the boy, what, then? You still think you can walk into a Cheyenne camp and take him?"

"I'll show you how we take the boy and escape. I've a blueprint for every step of it," Thorgard said.

Fargo let a wry sound escape his lips. "You've a blueprint for suicide," he said. "Don't include me in it."

"I need you. You're the only one that can track down the Cheyenne who has the boy," the man shouted. "You're the key to all the rest of it."

"Find another key," Fargo said, and turning, strode from the room. He pulled the door open, stepped outside, and felt the big man's frame at his heels.

"I'll double the money. Four thousand," Thorgard shouted.

Fargo continued walking to the Ovaro. "I've still only got one neck. I want to hang on to it a spell longer," he tossed back. "I'm out. Don't bother me anymore."

"No, you're in, Fargo," the man returned.

Fargo swung onto the Ovaro and paused to frown back at the man. "You really don't understand, do you?" he said. "Forget it. Find somebody else."

"I don't take no for an answer, Fargo. I get what I want, and I want you. I need you to find the boy," Thorgard boomed. "You're in. You'll be back."

"Hell I will," Fargo snapped, and sent the pinto into a canter. But he felt the frown dig into his forehead again as he rode. He wanted to dismiss the man as nothing more than an arrogant braggart, used to taking or buying whatever he wanted and now shouting empty words to take away the sting of defeat. But he knew better. Bertram Thorgard wasn't the kind for empty words. Underneath his arrogance was something else—a terrible darkness that gave his disdain an icy, searing edge.

But the man had no hold on him, Fargo reminded himself, none at all, and he wondered why he felt strangely uncomfortable as he rode through the dusk.

2

Night had descended when he reached Shadyville, and Fargo rode slowly into the town. The single, wide main street had already grown quiet, the Shadyville Saloon an oasis of noise as he rode past. He found the dry-goods store a little beyond the center of town, Vivian's name on a modest sign over the door. The lights were on inside and he dismounted, stepped to a partly curtained window, and peered into the store. He saw Vivian at once. A young girl stood near her, and Vivian's wide, pleasant face was drawn tight, her lips thin as she faced three men who were clearly out of place there.

All three wore dust-covered range outfits, worn and on the shabby side, and they each had the tight, small-featured faces of men who scrounged their way from place to place and job to job. The tallest of the trio wore a stained tan shirt and glowered threateningly at Vivian and the young girl. Fargo moved to the door, closed one hand around the doorknob, and slowly, silently eased the door open enough for him to hear.

"You were told to do somethin', sister. You'd better do it," Stained Shirt growled.

"I'll do what I want to do. Now get out," Vivian snapped, and turned to the young girl. "Put the new silks in their traveling boxes, Bessie," she said.

"Dammit, you do what you were told to do, or we take this place apart. You won't have anything to go anywhere with, honey," the man said. For emphasis, he swept three bolts of cotton goods from the counter with his arm.

"Get out, you stinking weasels," Vivian said. Fargo saw the fury in her eyes, her bodice push out as she drew a deep breath. She reached behind the counter and drew out a club as the man came toward her. He pulled back as she swung and missed his face by inches. But one of the other two, a thin, wiry man with a scar along one cheek, moved in on her from the side with quick, darting steps. Vivian tried to turn and bring the club up again, but he was too quick. The man had her pinned against the counter in moments.

"We'll teach you some manners, sister," Stained Shirt said, coming forward again.

Fargo pushed into the store, his voice cutting through the air with a quiet edge. "Let her go," he said, and the three men turned to face him. But he paused to take in the wide-eyed delight that flooded Vivian Keeler's face.

"Butt out, mister. Take off and be quick about it," Stained Shirt rasped.

Fargo sighed. "I'll say it one more time. Let her go," he repeated.

Stained Shirt flung a glance at the man holding Vivian. "Keep her there. We'll take care of this stupid bastard," he said, and the third man fell in step beside him as he came toward Fargo. He halted a few steps from the big man, who waited calmly. "You're lucky, mister," he said.

"How's that?" Fargo queried.

"We're just gonna break your face instead of killin' you," the man snarled. He lunged forward, threw a roundhouse, looping right as the other man attacked at the same time. Fargo pulled back, let the blow graze his chin, and stepped in, seized the man's arm, and spun him into the other figure.

"Goddamn," the other man snarled as he stumbled sideways. Fargo's quick, hard-driving left smashed into Stained Shirt's midsection, and the man doubled over, half-twisted away to cover up and avoid the follow-through blow. But Fargo's right hurtled over the man to slam into the other figure. The second attacker went backward, bounced off the counter, and fell to his knees. Fargo's glance went to Stained Shirt, and he saw the man start to straighten up. He brought his fist down in a hammerlike blow that landed on the back of the man's neck. The tan-shirted figure pitched face-forward to the floor, but Fargo's eyes had flicked past him before he landed. The second figure had pulled himself up, started to lunge forward, and now met a whistling left hook that spun him completely around. His chin hit the edge of the counter and he fell unconscious on the floor.

Fargo spun as the thin-framed figure holding Vivian pushed her away and yanked at the gun in his holster. Fargo drew, a motion swift as a diamondback's strike, his shot exploding even before the big Colt had leveled itself.

The man cursed in pain as he grabbed at his wrist,

suddenly, hanging from his arm in shattered limpness. The gun fell from his hand as he clutched his wrist. "Jesus, goddamn," the man cursed, pain in his voice. But there was fear in his eyes as he looked up at Fargo and the Colt aimed at him."No, don't . . . Jesus, no," he stammered.

"You're not worth two good bullets," Fargo said, and stepped back to the two figures still on the floor. He bent down, scooped up their guns, and tossed them on the counter. Vivian picked them up. "Open the door," he ordered.

The thin man protested. "Jesus, my wrist's broken. I can't use it."

"You've got another. Open the door," Fargo barked, and the man slid his thin frame toward the door. Fargo holstered the Colt, reached down, and picked up the two other figures by their shirt collars. He dragged them from the store as the thin one held the door open with one hand. Fargo flung the two men onto the ground and saw Stained Shirt stir, shake his head, and push himself onto one elbow. The man slowly came to, focusing on Fargo while his cohort remained unconscious.

"Jeez, I've got to find a sawbones," the thin one howled, holding his dangling wrist.

"You're lucky. Somebody could be finding an undertaker for you," Fargo said. "Hightail it, all of you. Don't come back unless you're tired of living."

Fargo watched Stained Shirt pick himself up and move toward the still-unconscious figure while the third man held his injured wrist to his side. There was no fight left in any of them, so he turned and went back into the store.

Vivian flew into his arms at once, her full-fleshed

figure warm against him. "God, you're a sight for sore eyes," she breathed.

"What was that all about?" he asked.

"Nothing important," she said, her dismissal too quick as she pulled back to survey him. "God, you look great," she said.

"Clean living," he remarked, and drew a short cry of protest from her.

"A lot of things could be keeping you looking so damn good, but that isn't one of them," Vivian said.

"You've too good a memory." Fargo laughed.

Vivian pulled him close again. "One of those memories is how you used to turn up whenever I needed help of some kind," she said fondly.

"Looks as if you're needing it again," Fargo said.

She pulled back. "No, not this time," Vivian said firmly, and turned to the young girl. "Fargo, this is Bessie, my assistant, the very best one you could ask for." Fargo watched the girl half-blush. "Go on home, Bessie. We'll finish packing in the morning," Vivian said, and Bessie included Fargo in a quick nod, as she disappeared behind the tall bolts of fabric.

Fargo's eyes took in Vivian as the woman turned back to him. He detected a few crows'-feet at the corners of her eyes, perhaps an extra ten pounds on hips and belly, but the pleasantly attractive face was there, the full, broad breasts still firm, her hair pulled back in a young girl's style. But most of all, the vibrant strength was still in the directness of her eyes and the defiant tilt of her head as she met his gaze.

"You're not just stopping by to turn around and leave," Vivian said with firmness.

"Is that an invite?" Fargo grinned.

"You know damn well what it is. Town stable's two

doors down the street. Go stable your horse and come around to the back door. That's where my living quarters are," Vivian said.

Fargo agreed with a nod, stepped from the store, and heard Vivian slip the bolt on the door behind him. He walked the Ovaro down to the town stable, where a small, grizzled little man came out to greet him. "Give him a good stall," Fargo said as he handed the reins to the stableman.

"The best for him," the man replied, taking in the striking Ovaro with an experienced eye.

Fargo left, returned to the back of the store, and knocked at the rear door. Vivian opened it and he followed her into a modest room, neat and well-kept with a sofa and chairs. He glimpsed a small hearth in an adjoining room and a third room, containing a big brass bed.

Vivian handed him a shot glass of deep amber liquid. "Bourbon," she said smugly.

"That memory again." He laughed, drank deep of the liquid, and felt its rich smoothness.

Vivian sipped from her glass and came to him. She reached up and let her lips press against his in a long, warm kiss made of old memories and new desires. She pulled back again, sipping from her drink again as he downed his.

"You want to tell me what that was all about before?" he asked her.

"No," she said. "I'm handling it."

"You could've fooled me," he remarked evenly. "Looks to me like you're pulling out."

"Yes," Vivian said, and he caught the tightness in the single word.

"Why?" he pressed.

"I've my reasons," she said. "I don't want to talk about it. I don't want to waste time with you finally here in front of me. I just want to turn back clocks. God, how often I've thought about you coming this way sometime." Vivian's lips found his at once—warm and wet and moving against his mouth.

"You've been alone too long, I'd say," Fargo murmured.

"Too long," she agreed. "You know I've never been one for taking up quick and easy, and here, where I've the store, it just hasn't seemed right to do." Her hands came up, pressed against both sides of his face, moved slowly as though she were trying to imprint him on her through touch. "You being here is making me explode inside."

He felt the fire of her in her fingertips and saw the explosion of desire in the way her eyes devoured his face. He rose with her as she stood up suddenly, pulled him toward her, and crossed to the bedroom. She spun away, unbuttoned clasps, and yanked the dress over her head, spun toward him again in long pink bloomers and a bodice that just barely contained the broad, deep breasts.

"You always were impatient." Fargo laughed as he pulled off clothes. "I've a memory, too."

"Only with you," she said, pulling the bodice free. The broad breasts gushed forward, brown-pink tips on light-brown circles. She all but flung herself onto the wide bed, yanked off bloomers, turned up a round, full bottom for an instant, and rolled onto her back, her eyes on Fargo. The thick black triangle pushed up at him and her rounded belly jiggled as she moved. Her fire reached out and he felt himself responding, stiffening as he shed the last of his clothes and he was beside the bed in one long, eager stride, sinking down atop her, pressing himself onto the very soft, pillowy breasts. He felt the full-fleshed thighs lift, press hard against his sides, and his lips closed over one brown-pink nipple, tasting its soft firmness as Vivian's hand pushed her other breast against the side of his face.

"Yes, yes, oh, Jesus, yes," he heard her cry out, and her belly rose up under him, pushed hard against his throbbing maleness, a wild plea curled in her voice. All the full womanliness of her rose up for him, pulled and pushed at him, thighs of soft flesh clasping around him, broad pillowed breasts quivering for his mouth, rounded, soft pubic mound burning through the hard fibers of the black triangle. "Take me, God, take me, take me, oh, God, Fargo, I'm on fire," Vivian cried out, and her hands pounded against his back.

Vivian had always been fiercely direct, never one for subtleties, and now the driving hunger inside her added to it. He rose, drew back, found her flowing warm moistness, and plunged forward. "Oh, oh, oh, aaaaah, Fargo, Jesus, Jesus, oh, yes," she screamed. Her thighs slammed against his ribs, fell open, slammed back again as she pushed upward. He thrust hard inside her, pulled back, thrust again as she cried out for more, wanting the harshness, the deep roughness of his lovemaking as flesh responded to flesh, desire governing their actions.

"Again, God, again," Vivian cried out in a rasping voice as he rammed deep and felt the warm walls enclose him. He paused, drew back, and began to increase his tempo with a suddenness beyond his control. Vivian's little gasped cry rose and he felt her breasts quiver, shake from side to side as his face stayed buried in the encompassing softness. "Yes, yes, now, now, oh, God, now . . . it's now," Vivian gasped, her cry a low, hoarse sound, and her body quaked under him, shook, and seemed possessed. Her thighs locked around him, held, and her moan spiraled to trail off in hoarse gasps as despair followed ecstasy. "Oh, more, more . . . damn," Vivian half-sobbed, and her legs clung to him, refused to let him go. He stayed with her, enjoying the aftermath of rapture inside her warmth. Her deep, strained breathing finally slowed and grew even.

He stayed with her until she moved at last, gave him up with a broken sigh, and pulled his head against her broad breasts. "You sure were hungering, honey," Fargo said.

"Been thinking a lot about you. Maybe I worked myself up, and suddenly you're here," Vivian said, moving to let him sit up and look at her.

"Maybe," he said. "But whatever the reasons, it was sure worth the coming here. For me, anyway."

"And for me. It was always worth it for me. You know that," Vivian said, lay back, and one broad breast fell against his chest. "I've never forgotten all the things you did for me after Frank died, Fargo. Little things and big things—sometimes the little ones were more important to me than the big ones. You got me through a very hard time."

"But when you left, you came here and made it on your own. I'd say you've done real well here, Vivian," he answered.

"I have," she admitted.

"Then why are you pulling out?" he tossed in sharply, and watched her face quickly stiffen.

"Sometimes you have to move on," she said.

"Leave a good thing you've built up? That's a big price for pulling up stakes," Fargo commented.

"Everything has a price. The price of staying on is too high for me to live with. A matter of conscience, maybe. So I'm moving on," Vivian said.

"You're holding back on me, honey," Fargo commented.

"I just don't want to talk about it. I'll go on and find someplace else," she said.

"Sounded earlier as though somebody doesn't want that," he observed.

"Too bad," she sniffed.

"Nothing more you want to tell me?" he prodded.

She turned, and the broad, soft breasts brushed against his chest as her arms slid around his neck. "Yes, make love to me again," she murmured.

"I never say no to a lady," he answered, and his head lowered, his mouth finding one soft breast. He drew in the softly firm tip, and Vivian instantly groaned in pleasure. He made love to her again and she was only a little less impatient this time, her full, womanly body responding with absolute totality, every breathing, pulsating fiber of her reveling in sheer pleasure. Later, she slept beside him and he enjoyed the good feel of a warm woman's body against him.

She woke with him when morning came, and frowned at the new day. "Usually I don't mind seeing the morning come. Today I'm sorry," she muttered, swinging from the bed. He watched her full, white, round rear bounce as she hurried across the room. He let her wash and dress first, and she made coffee as he rose. He finished washing up and joined her in the kitchen, where she handed him a mug of the steaming liquid.

"You've a town all picked out for yourself?" he asked.

"No, but I've no more stomach for pioneer towns. I was thinking of heading east, finding someplace a little civilized," Vivian said, tossing him a speculative glance over the rim of her coffee mug. "You could come along, for a little while. That'd sure make it all worthwhile," she offered.

"Maybe." He shrugged. "If you leveled with me. You've got to have a damn good reason for walking away from a good business, Vivian."

"I told you, I do. That'll have to be enough," she said with a touch of crossness.

A bell jangled in the store and she rose, opening a door that led out of her living quarters to the front of the store. "That'll be Bessie. I'll let her in," she said as she hurried away.

Fargo finished the coffee, rose, and walked into the store, where Vivian gave the girl packing instructions for a dozen bolts of cotton goods. "When do you figure to be packed to go?" he asked.

"By tonight," she said. "Come with me. There's nothing to keep you around here."

"That's true enough," he admitted. "I'll think some on it while I'm currying the Ovaro. He needs a good grooming. Be back later."

Vivian blew him a quick kiss and turned to the packing boxes that lined one wall. Fargo walked from the store, paused outside in the sun, and let his eyes sweep the street before he strode on to the stable. The old stableman brought the magnificent Ovaro out to him at once, patting the powerful jet-black neck with one hand.

"Miss Vivian was right," he said admiringly.

"Miss Vivian?" Fargo frowned.

"She said I'd maybe get to see one of the finest pintos I'll ever see," the old man said.

Fargo stared at the stableman as an explosion of thoughts circled in his head. "She said that, did she?" he murmured.

"Yep, and she was sure right. That's some fine horse," the man said.

Fargo nodded and paid the stableman. The small furrow stayed on his brow as he led the horse back to the dry-goods store. He dropped the reins over a rail and Vivian looked up in surprise as he entered the store. "Take a break, Bessie," Fargo said to the young girl. "Your boss and I have some talking to do."

Vivian frowned at him as he took her by the elbow and propelled her toward the back of the store. "What're you doing, Fargo? What's all this about?" she protested.

"It's about lying and telling fancy tales," he said. "You didn't work yourself up thinking about me. You knew I'd be here. You told the stableman about the Ovaro."

Her lips tightened. "That old big-mouth," she muttered.

"Only one other person expected I'd show up here," Fargo snapped. "Bertram Thorgard, and that tells me something else too."

"What?" she asked, and met his eyes boldly.

"It tells me Bertram Thorgard has something to do with you pulling up stakes. Now, I want the damn truth of it, Vivian," Fargo boomed.

Vivian's wide, pleasant face stayed set for another few moments, but a half-angry sigh finally escaped her. "He owns this building. He told me he'd triple my rent and toss me out on the street. There's no other place I can go, seeing as how he owns all the other buildings in town," Vivian said. "All so I'd get you to ride trail for him. He'd learned we were good friends once. He figured you wouldn't let that happen to me if I told you."

"So I'd ride trail for him for your sake," Fargo finished, and Vivian nodded. "Why didn't you tell me?" he asked.

"I couldn't ask that of you, Fargo—pressure you to get yourself killed chasing that grandson of his because of me," Vivian said.

"So you decided to pull up stakes on your own," Fargo said.

"That's right. I figured he couldn't do anything about that. It solved everything, for you and for me," Vivian answered. "Then yesterday he sent those three vultures to tell me they'd leave me nothing to pull out with if I tried to go on my own."

Fargo's lips formed a thin line as his thoughts rested on Bertram Thorgard. "The bastard doesn't miss a trick, does he?" he muttered. "He'll use anyone and anything to get his way."

"Only this time it won't work. I'm pulling out with everything I own," Vivian said.

"It'll work," Fargo said grimly. "I can't let you walk away from all the years of work here, of building up a business, everything you have here because of me."

"What about all the times you helped me?" Vivian countered.

"Not the same. I wasn't tossing away years of work to do it," Fargo said, and Bertram Thorgard swam into his thoughts again. The man wouldn't get his way at his price. He'd have to pay for it, Fargo murmured silently. "Draw up a letter of agreement between yourself and Thorgard," he said to Vivian. "Do it right now. Let it say that he agrees not to raise your rent for the next twenty-five years or bother you and your business in any way."

Vivian's eyes were wide as she stared at him. "He'll never sign such a thing," she said.

"He'll sign," Fargo said. "Do it. I'll be waiting outside for you." He left her, strode from the store, and went to the post where the Ovaro waited. He took a body brush from his saddlebag and proceeded to give the pinto a quick brushing. He had just finished when Vivian came out, the envelope in one hand.

"I've a buckboard," she said.

"Get it," he said, and waited until she returned driving the light rig. He swung in beside her and rode tight-jawed toward the Thorgard spread. He took the envelope from Vivian as they halted in front of the house and Thorgard opened the door for them. Fargo stepped inside, Vivian a half-stride behind him, and he saw the smugness of victory in Bertram Thorgard's cold smile.

"I told you you'd be back, Fargo," the man said.

"So you did," Fargo agreed.

"You wouldn't let the little lady sacrifice everything for you. That's not your style," Thorgard said. "I do my homework and I know people. That's why I always get what I want. That's why I'll get my grandson back."

Fargo let a wry snort escape his lips. "You ever know the Cheyenne?" he asked.

"I'm prepared," Thorgard said.

"You better be prepared for a hell of a lot of surprises," Fargo commented, handing the envelope to the man. "Start with this one," he said.

Thorgard took the sheet of paper from the envelope and a frown slid across his face as he read from it. He looked up at Fargo when he finished. "This your price?" he asked.

"This, and the money," Fargo said.

"Ridiculous. The money's more than enough," Thorgard said. "You can throw this away."

Fargo shrugged. "You don't sign, I don't trail," Fargo said evenly.

Bertram Thorgard's eyes held the anger of a man unaccustomed to being outmaneuvered at his own game, and his jutting jaw throbbed. Fargo waited another long, silent moment and started to turn away with Vivian. "Hold on," Thorgard bit out, and Fargo halted. He watched the man stride halfway across the room to a table where an inkwell and quill pen rested at one side. He snatched up the pen and scrawled his name on the agreement with an angry flourish. "Here," he half-snarled at Vivian. "Take your goddamn agreement and get out of my sight."

Fargo smiled as they walked to the buckboard, and she clung to him for a long moment. "I'll be waiting, whenever you get back," she murmured. "Be careful, Fargo, please be careful."

"I plan on that," he replied. He waited until she drove from the ranch before returning to the house.

"You drive a hard bargain, Fargo," Thorgard said then. "But I still won."

"You win on other people's backs. That's not hard," Fargo returned.

"I win. That's all I care about," Thorgard said. "Now,

I'll introduce you to the rest of the men who'll be riding with us."

Fargo followed the man outside where he sent his booming voice across to the bunkhouses and the stables. The Trailsman watched as the figures emerged and drew closer. Fargo counted sixty-five men as they gathered in a half-circle. A sizable little army, Fargo noted, but Thorgard would need them all for what he planned.

Skye surveyed the group with a slow glance. A shiftless, raunchy lot, he observed silently, drifters and the displaced, every one of them carrying the mark of shiftless wanderers in their hard-bitten faces and darting eyes.

One, a tall, well-built man with thin lips and slitted eyes, stepped forward. "Frank Dallison," Thorgard introduced. "Frank's in charge, under my direction, of course." He started to say more when a three-spring grocery wagon rolled into the yard. "Those are the extra supplies I ordered. I'll have to check them out. You two can get acquainted, meanwhile."

As Thorgard swung onto the wagon and rode it into one of the barns, Frank Dallison speared Fargo with a cold stare from his narrow, slitted eyes. "You don't look special to me, mister," Dallison said.

"Sorry about that," Fargo said pleasantly.

"We've been waiting around for you to show up, and I don't like waiting," Dallison growled.

"I'm all upset about that," Fargo said, his voice growing colder.

"You just make sure you follow orders," Dallison said.

"I don't follow orders, cousin. I work alone in my own way," Fargo answered.

"I'm in charge. You heard Thorgard," the man said.

"Of that collection of pack rats, not me," Fargo snapped.

"Maybe you'd like me to show you who's boss right now," Dallison said, and a cold smile edged his lips.

Fargo hesitated a moment. Backing away from Dallison's type only meant more trouble. He'd take any retreat as weakness, and that only meant putting off the inevitable showdown.

"Why don't you do that, stupid," Fargo said quietly. He turned to face the man squarely.

A moment of surprise touched Dallison's face, and then a half-sneer of cold confidence spread across his lips. He moved forward, his hands lifting, and Fargo half-circled. Dallison threw a fast left, but Fargo saw it for the feint it was and pulled away from the right that followed. The man tried another feint with no more success. But he had fast hands, Fargo noted as he circled to his left and let Dallison come in on him again. This time Dallison flicked out three quick left jabs and Fargo slipped away from each, was ready for the right that shot forward, and ducked the blow.

Skye continued to move back as he circled and let himself seem tentative. He watched Dallison's sneering confidence grow instantly. The man threw two more blows and Fargo countered with two punches that were slow and Dallison blocked with ease. The man's slitted eyes bored into him as he came forward again, less carefully now. He threw a left and a right, both hard, whistling blows, and followed with a wild swinging left that Fargo pulled away from with his own quickness. He seemed to waver uncertainly and Dallison leapt in with a tremendous left cross that almost landed. But the blow left him with all his weight on one foot as he half-turned off balance. Fargo's right came around with a sudden explosion of power and speed to smash into the man's ribs with bone-rattling force.

Dallison grunted in pain as he doubled over sideways. He never saw the whistling left fist that came up in a low arc and smashed into his jaw. His head swiveled as he went back and down, hitting the ground with a tremendous thud to lay still. Fargo straightened, looked down as Dallison moved, tried to turn, and fell back onto the ground again. He watched as the man slowly rolled onto his side, still dazed, shook his head, and lay there.

The fight was over, Fargo knew. For now. Dallison had learned a lesson. But he wasn't the kind to let it stop there. He'd pick another time, another place, to reestablish himself, at a moment when he'd be sure to give himself the edge on success. That was the pattern of Dallison's kind. Fargo put aside the thought, knowing he'd have to be ready for that moment.

Fargo turned as Thorgard strode from the barn, his heavy face darkening at once as he saw Dallison slowly starting to pick himself up from the ground. "What the hell's going on here?" Thorgard boomed.

"You said get acquainted," Fargo answered, and Thorgard glared at him.

"Come with me," the man said, and strode into the house with Fargo following. Thorgard whirled to face him. "Dammit, I need every one of those men out there, especially Frank Dallison. I don't want you starting trouble."

"I didn't start it. I just finished it," Fargo said.

"I don't care. I don't want trouble. I want them

saving their energies for the Cheyenne," Thorgard said.

"Then tell Dallison to stay clear of me. I don't want any part of the scurvy lot of them," Fargo snapped.

"I picked every one of them and I'm paying them good money," Bertram Thorgard said with a touch of righteousness.

Fargo's laugh was a harsh sound. "Yes, and I know why you picked them," he said.

"What's that supposed to mean?" The man frowned.

"They're not Indian fighters. They won't stand a chance against the Cheyenne," Fargo said. "They're throwaway bodies, hired to die, to give the Cheyenne something to shoot at. And they're all too damn dumb to know it."

Bertram Thorgard's eyes grew ice-cold. "You do your job and keep your goddamn opinions to yourself, Fargo, understand?" he thundered.

"Relax. I'm not aiming to make any speeches to them," Fargo said. "But that's not opinion, that's truth, and you're still a bastard, Thorgard. Maybe you're a fourteen-carat one, but you're a bastard."

"You be ready to ride, come dawn. I'll fill you in on everything you have to know, then," Thorgard said, and strode from the room.

Fargo half-smiled to himself as he sauntered toward the front door. He had almost reached it when a voice containing a tinge of amusement cut into his thoughts.

"Very impressive," it said, and he turned to see the tall, willowy form, sandy hair loosely framing a high-cheekboned face with a straight nose, finely edged lips, and hazel-flecked, green eyes. It was a most attractive face, faint amusement still dancing in the green eyes.

"Which? Outside or inside?" he asked.

She half-shrugged. "Both," she said, and he saw longish breasts that curved up from full cups to press against a pale-green shirt. A black riding skirt outlined flat hips, a flat belly, and the long, slow curve of firm legs. "Most people don't talk to Bertram Thorgard that way, much less beat him at anything," she said.

"I'm not most people," Fargo remarked.

"Obviously," she said, and her smile was sudden, flashing warmth with a touch of ruefulness in it.

"How do you know so much about Bertram Thorgard, honey?" Fargo asked.

"Daughters learn about their fathers the hard way. I'm April Thorgard," she said.

Fargo felt his brows lift. "Sorry, but I'm not taking back anything I said about him," he told her.

"You shouldn't. I'm sure you were absolutely right. But he's made his plans carefully, spent a lot of money, and used all his connections. Don't underestimate him."

"I know better than that," Fargo agreed, and his eyes narrowed as he studied April Thorgard. "You sound like something less than the devoted daughter," he remarked.

A tiny half-smile touched the finely edged lips. "Right, again," she said. "But I suppose I shouldn't be surprised after the way you read my dear father."

"There are all kinds of signs," he said. "Some on trails, some on people."

A touch of bitterness crept into her half-smile. "There are, indeed. I haven't lived here in almost ten years. Father hasn't changed a bit, except now he's even more ruthless," she said. Fargo saw April Thorgard take in the chiseled power of his face, the muscled hardness of his body. "I'm glad you're going. Maybe he'll have a change to pull this off with you along," she said.

"You switch signals fast, honey," Fargo said. "Coldness, first, and now concern for him."

"No concern for him. Pure selfishness. My neck will be on the line, too," the young woman said.

"What?" Fargo blurted.

"He's bringing me along," she said, and the bitterness was suddenly strong in her voice.

"Is he altogether crazy?" Fargo spit out. "Bringing his own daughter along on this?"

"He feels the boy must be kept quiet and in hand after he's taken back, and only the soothing comfort and tenderness of a woman's touch can do that. I've been elected. The care of the boy on the way back will be my responsibility," April Thorgard said.

"He's crazy. He already lost one daughter to the Cheyenne and now he's going to risk another?" Fargo frowned.

"He only cares about what he wants. You said as much yourself," she replied.

"Then you're crazy to go along with it," Fargo said.

April shrugged and the long breasts lifted, touched tiny points against the pale-green shirt. "You're here," she said.

"You heard why," he snapped.

"The woman must mean a lot to you," she observed.

"Not the way you're thinking. She was being done in on my account, and that meant a lot to me," Fargo answered.

"No matter. You still made a choice. I didn't have that luxury," April said.

"Why not? You said you hadn't lived here in ten years."

"A long story. Besides, that's none of your concern," she said, her chin lifting. "I'm here and I'm going and I don't like it, but there's nothing can be done about that except make the best of it."

"I'm thinking the Cheyenne are going to make the best of it," Fargo replied, turning as he started to stride from the room. He paused at the door and looked back at April Thorgard. She held her high-cheekboned face expressionless and somehow managed to appear both really cool and quietly hurt, all wrapped in loveliness. "He's got no damn business bringing you on this. I don't care what damn reason he has, and I'm going to tell him so," Fargo said.

"Don't waste you breath, Fargo," April said, and he knew she was right. He turned, angry, pulled the door open. "One thing more," she said, and he paused. "Nothing is the way it seems with Bertram Thorgard, and he always has a hole card. That's his way. That's why he always wins."

"Thanks for the advice." Fargo nodded and went out into the gathering dusk. Her advice was also a warning, he thought with a frown. And something more, something she didn't dare spell out. She held a fear of her father inside her, along with a mixture of bitterness and hurt. But he sensed a quiet strength to her, too. Maybe she'd be more than just trouble. Maybe she'd make the whole stinking trip worthwhile. Maybe.

He paused beside the Ovaro, the furrow still deep in his brow as he thought about Bertram Thorgard. The man had to be insane to bring April along. Or maybe he didn't give a damn about her. Maybe there was no love lost between either of them. Yet Thorgard seemed to have some hold over her. She was here, doing his bidding, Fargo had to admit as he pulled himself onto the horse.

He started to turn the Ovaro when he saw April walk from the house in the purple haze of the dusk. She moved with the grace of a cattail swaying in a marsh breeze, a smooth sinuousness to her. Thorgard was still a thoroughly selfish bastard to bring her along, Fargo muttered silently as he turned to ride from the ranch.

He passed half a dozen figures near the bunkhouse and saw Frank Dallison detach himself from the others. "A lucky punch, Fargo." The man sneered, and Fargo knew the bluster in his voice was meant for those standing nearby. "Next time it'll be different," Dallison threatened.

"Definitely," Fargo agreed, catching the flash of uncertainty in the man's eyes as he moved on.

Darkness fell as Skye rode from the ranch. He found a low hill and a place to bed down under a shagbark hickory. April Thorgard hung in his thoughts. She had been more than a surprise. She was a question mark of her own, and strange undercurrents were suddenly present. They'd been there in her cryptic advice, a warning edged with the hint of dark and hidden things. Thorgard's plan to snatch a boy from the midst of the Cheyenne was lunacy enough. Now it had taken on new and veiled dimensions. He'd damn well find out what they were before it was too late to matter, Fargo murmured as sleep crept up on him at last.

3

The full complement of Thorgards' hired guns were ready to move out, most already on their horses, as Fargo rode into the ranch the next day. The man waited in front of the main house, arrogant determination in his heavy face. Fargo dismounted and met Thorgard's eyes. The man clipped out sentences as though it were an effort to speak.

"The attack took place just north of the headwaters of the Powder River," he said. "It was led by a Cheyenne called Thunderhawk."

"That's it? That's all you have?" Fargo frowned.

"A place and a name. That's something to go on," Thorgard said, and bristled.

"It's goddamn little," Fargo said, and stared into space for a moment. He finally returned his eyes to Thorgard. "It'll take you a few days to reach the Powder. Make camp just below Hell's Half Acre. I'll meet you there," he said.

"Where are you going?" Thorgard frowned.

"Look up old friends and ask new questions," Fargo

said, and saw April come out of the house. The hazel-flecked eyes met his gaze with contained coolness as she halted. Fargo felt Thorgard's frown on him and turned his gaze back to the man. "You afraid I'll run out on you?" he asked.

"No, that's not your style," Thorgard said. "But you'll take your own sweet time. You might even look up an old girlfriend along the way, and I don't want that."

'You on a timetable?" Fargo questioned.

"Of sorts," Thorgard said.

Fargo glanced at April. "I'll take her with me. She'll see that I don't waste time," he said.

"No," Thorgard snapped instantly. "April rides with me. You just get there damn quickly, Fargo." He turned and strode away to where Frank Dallison and the others waited.

"Nice try," Fargo heard April say, and a tiny light of amusement danced in the hazel-flecked eyes.

"Nice try for what?" Fargo asked mildly.

"At a chance to ask me more questions," she said. "You don't want a watchdog along. You want more answers."

He smiled. "Maybe I just like pretty company," he said.

She fastened him with a wry glance. "At the risk of sounding indelicate, bullshit," she said.

"You underestimate yourself," he remarked.

A tiny smile touched the finely edged lips. "Maybe you'll get another chance," she said, and walked on toward the stable.

Fargo watched her for a moment, her flat, tight bottom hardly moving under the riding skirt. He turned and climbed onto the Ovaro as she disappeared into the stable. Skye rode past Thorgard as the man and Frank Dallison gathered with the others, then he turned the pinto northeast and set a steady pace that the sturdy horse took without drawing a labored breath. By dusk he had skirted the Green Mountains and turned east toward Medicine Bow. He bedded down for the night in a glen of peachleaf willow and his body welcomed sleep. But he was in the saddle with the dawn and forged the North Platte by noon. He rode past a collection of shacks, a supply store, and a saloon that called itself a town. He continued on into a gentle valley of American elm and hackberry.

It had been years, but everything was suddenly familiar, the narrow passageway all but invisible at the end of the valley, marked by the bent elm that led to the tiny cul-de-sac of silver balsam. He slowed, peered ahead, searched for the little shack, and found it, even more hidden than he'd remembered. He heard the woman's voice first, chattering in Siouan, and then he spotted the two figures in front of the shack. Albert Twopenny was unmistakable in his old, battered fedora and baggy army trousers. A young girl in a deerskin dress with the sawtooth-cut bottom of the Hidatsa stood beside him.

Albert Twopenny turned as Fargo came through the trees, and a wide smile of astonishment covered the broad, flat-cheekboned face that was still amazingly free of wrinkles. The product of two tribal families, Albert Twopenny had inherited the best of both.

"Fargo!" the old Indian cried out."By damn. Son of a gun." He took a step forward, winced, and Fargo saw the bandage wrapped around the bottom of one leg. Fargo dropped from the saddle as Albert Twopenny hobbled forward and clenched hands with him.

Skye noted that the old man's grip was still strong. "You damn sight for sore eyes, Fargo," Albert said happily.

"You, too, Albert, you old fox," Fargo returned. He shot a glance at the girl and saw black hair worn in two long braids, a young face with black eyes, even, pretty features, a nose small for an Indian girl, and bronze-tinted, smooth skin. The girl surveyed him with curiosity and he returned his gaze to Albert Twopenny. "What happened to your leg?" he asked.

"Bad fall, came down on ax," the old Indian said. "Take long time to get better." He gestured to the girl. "This is Little Flower. You would call her a niece. She is from my father's people."

"Hidatsa," Fargo said, and Albert smiled broadly.

"You always have damn good memory, Fargo," he said. "She comes every month since I hurt my leg."

"To help this stubborn old man get his supplies," the girl said bluntly.

"What was all the shouting about?" Fargo inquired.

"She cannot go to town alone anymore. They will not let her get away this time," Albert Twopenny said sternly.

"Who?" Fargo asked.

"In town, bad ones, very bad. Just hang around all the time. They almost take her last time she go," Albert said.

Fargo looked at the girl. "Is this so?" he asked.

Her pretty features took on a thin veil of truculence. "Yes, but I ran from them last time. I can do it again," she said.

"They tell her they wait for her next time. They are always there. Coyotes. She cannot go alone," Albert Twopenny cut in.

Little Flower looked at him with disdain. "And how will you help me? You can hardly walk. They will just kill you," she said.

"I can shoot. Albert Twopenny is not a helpless old man," Albert answered, and Fargo heard the pride as well as the hurt in his voice.

"Never, not you, old friend," Fargo said soothingly. "But there is wisdom and there is foolish pride. You, the greatest scout the Third Cavalry ever had, know that."

Albert Twopenny let his silence agree reluctantly. "I can do without fresh supplies," he said.

"No, you can't," Little Flower contradicted immediately.

"Silence," Albert Twopenny thundered. "You are a chattering magpie. My old friend Fargo did not come here to hear this. He has come to talk to me about something."

"You talk. I'll get the supplies. I'll be all right," the girl said, and strode away.

Albert started to call to her, but he held back as Fargo lifted his hand and she disappeared around the back of the shack.

"She wants to help you. She has her pride, too," Fargo half-whispered. "She does not want you hurt. Let her go. I will follow her."

"I cannot ask that of you Fargo," Albert Twopenny whispered.

"How many times have we helped each other, old friend?" Fargo chided. "I have things to ask you, but we will talk about those later."

He broke off as Little Flower appeared on a sturdy gray burro, the deerskin dress riding high on her legs to reveal beautifully curved calves and smooth knees.

She dug her heels into the burro's side and trotted past without a bounce or a jiggle. She had a tight, controlled body, Fargo decided as he watched her vanish through the trees.

He waited until he was certain she had gone through the narrow passage before turning the Ovaro to follow. "I'll bring her back, Albert," he murmured, and slowly rode away. He hung back, emerged from the passageway onto the end of the valley, and stayed in the trees as he glimpsed the little burro ahead of him. The girl rode slowly and steadily. Finally, when she had left the long valley, he followed inside a line of silver fir and saw the town come into sight. He slowed, let Little Flower ride in on the burro, and then sent the Ovaro into a fast trot. He steered behind the line of ramshackle structures and reined to a halt when he spied the burro outside the supply store.

The saloon bordered the supply store, he noted. Little Flower appeared with two sacks, slung them over the burro, and returned to the store. Fargo felt his eyes narrowing as he saw the four figures drift out of the saloon, two halting by the burro, the other two taking up positions on both sides. They were saloon rats, he saw—pasty-faced, scurvy types, three sporting a week's stubble. The fourth one had a face marked with the tiny network of red veins that signaled the constant drinker.

Fargo took hold of his lariat. He'd only use the big Colt if he had to, he told himself, and leaned forward in the saddle as Little Flower emerged to put two more sacks over the burro.

"Well, look who's come back," the one with the red-veined face said, and stepped toward the burro.

Little Flower ignored him as she adjusted the sacks on the burro. "I'm talking to you, squaw," he growled.

Little Flower finished tying the sacks in silence.

"She doesn't want to talk to us," one of the others said, a gangly figure with sallow skin.

"Well, she don't have to talk. All she's gonna have to do is give us some squaw pussy," the other said. He exploded in a surprisingly quick dive that let him wrap long arms around the girl.

She kicked and tried to pull away from him, but he lifted her up while the sallow-faced one came in to seize her left arm and twist it behind her. Fargo heard Little Flower gasp in pain as they walked behind her, each holding one arm while pushing toward one of the ramshackle huts. The other two fell in beside them.

"I get it first," the red-veined face said, and Fargo saw Little Flower bend her head and try to sink her teeth into his arm, but he yanked her head up and she cried out in pain.

Fargo wheeled the Ovaro and sent the horse into a full gallop around the building. He had the lariat whirling as he raced into the open and saw the two men holding Little Flower glance up in surprise. But the lasso was in midair, circling down over them, and Fargo pulled it tight instantly. The noose, around both their necks, yanked them into each other as Fargo pulled hard on it. Their heads came together with a resounding crash as Little Flower broke free and fell forward. Fargo held the lasso taut as both men collapsed on the ground and he skidded the Ovaro to a halt.

His eyes were on the other two and he saw one yank at his gun. Even though he had to switch the lariat to his left hand, Fargo had the big Colt out of its holster and ready to fire before the man could bring his gun up. The Colt barked and the third man cursed in pain as the bullet went through his arm and smashed his elbow. His gun fell to the ground as Fargo's lake-blue eyes speared the fourth man, who stumbled backward, tripped over his own feet, and fell, stark terror in his eyes. "No, don't, mister . . . I was just standin' by," he stammered.

"Picking the wrong friends can get a man killed," Fargo said.

"No, Jesus, don't kill me," the man begged.

Fargo dropped from the pinto, his eyes on the man. "Throw your gun over here, nice and slow," he said, and the man obeyed, skittered the gun along the ground. Fargo picked it up and saw Little Flower moving closer to him. He stepped to where the other two still lay dazedly on the ground, the lasso around their necks. Pulling the lariat free, Fargo took their guns and threw all three of the weapons over the roof of the nearest shack. He waited and let the two men shake their heads clear. When he saw their eyes begin to focus on him and one push himself to a sitting position, he stepped forward. "You hear me, you stinking bastards?" he rumbled.

The one with the red-veined face managed a nod as the sallow-skinned one blinked away the last of his dizziness. They were all hollow men, quick to bully and equally quick to cower, and like all their kind, they had the rodent's sense of when to be afraid.

Fargo saw the fear in their eyes. "You ever touch her again and you're dead men. You can count on it," he said. "You understand?"

The sallow-skinned one nodded, but the other one

held truculence in his eyes along with fear. They were weasels, but fear wouldn't be enough for them. They had to remember out of pain that couldn't be wiped away by hollow bluster.

Fargo's motion was quick—the Colt raised and a single shot fired and the red-veined face contorted in a scream of pain as the man's kneecap shattered.

"Owwwoooo, Jesus, oh, God," he cried out as he rolled across the ground, clutching at his leg.

Fargo swept the others with a glance. The one with the splintered elbow sat on the ground and rocked back and forth as he held his arm, and the other two stared at him in terror. Skye holstered the Colt. They'd remember the promise of pain. He turned, gestured to Little Flower, and she pulled herself onto the burro, following him as he slowly rode from the excuse for a town.

She rode in silence until he entered the gentle valley and then she prodded the burro to come alongside him and he slowed the Ovaro to a walk. "Why didn't you say you were going to follow me?" she asked, and he caught the hint of a glower in her black eyes.

"You'd have argued again," he said, and she stared straight ahead. "I am right. You know it," he said.

"Yes," she admitted with a tiny smile, and turned her pretty face to him again with a tinge of admiration in it."You are all that Albert Twopenny has said about you," she remarked. "He has often talked of his friend, Fargo, the white trailsman with the wisdom of the owl and the cunning of the mountain lion."

"Albert likes to tell stories," Fargo said.

"No, no stories," she said, her eyes studying him. "I was wrong to think I could get away from them. You knew better. They would have taken me, perhaps killed me afterward."

"Lessons are to be remembered," Fargo said.

"And good deeds are to be rewarded," she said. "That is our way. You know this."

"There's no need to talk of that," Fargo said as they rode into the tree-lined passageway and emerged to see Albert seated on a stump outside his hut. Little Flower was already telling him what had happened as she hopped from the burro. When she finished, the old scout pinned her with a grim gaze.

"Maybe you will learn to listen to your elders now," he said. "Take the supplies inside."

Little Flower nodded obediently and Fargo followed Albert into the hut, whose interior, covered with hides and bearskin rugs, resembled a tepee more than it did a house. Albert brought out a jug and handed it to Fargo as they sat on the floor on a bearskin rug.

"Good whiskey," Fargo said, talking a deep sip of rich Kentucky rye. He sat back patiently and let Albert Twopenny talk of many things, old times and old stories and new wisdoms. It was the custom, the old way. Abruptness was considered impolite, and Fargo reminisced along with him until Albert finally fastened him with a speculative stare. "And now you have come to visit with me, old friend. Why?" he asked. "I have not scouted for years."

"But you have not sat here like a mushroom. I know better than that. You have ridden the hills, talked, listened, watched. You know what the wind sighs, Albert Twopenny," Fargo said, and the old scout's impassive face almost smiled. Fargo glanced up as Little Flower brought in the last of the supplies and folded herself into a corner of the room. "I want to know about a warrior called Thunderhawk," Fargo said to Albert.

The old Indian's eyes widened a fraction. "Yes, I know of this Thunderhawk. He is a fierce warrior. It is said he has never lost a battle," Albert answered.

"He is a Cheyenne, I am told," Fargo said.

"Wind River Cheyenne," Albert said, and Fargo's eyes narrowed at once.

"Then his camp will be in the Wind River Mountains," Fargo said, and Albert nodded.

"Five years ago he led an attack on a wagon train. Did you hear about it? He took a little boy," Fargo said.

"I have heard nothing about that. But he took the woman with the yellow hair," Albert said.

"That would be the boy's mother," Fargo said.

"He make her one of his wives, it is said," Albert answered.

"You mean one of his slaves," Fargo corrected.

"I mean one of his wives," the old man repeated firmly. "He make many Cheyenne angry by that, but they were too afraid of Thunderhawk to speak out. But yellow-hair wife die, two, maybe three years later." Albert Twopenny paused, fastened Fargo with a shrewd glance. "You do not ask about Thunderhawk for yourself," he remarked.

"No, I've been hired to find him. But the Wind River Range is a big place. It could take too long to track him down," Fargo said. "What else can you tell me, Albert?"

"I stay away from the Wind River Cheyenne," Albert said. "But Little Flower passes along the edge of the mountains to return to her people."

Fargo turned his gaze on the girl and she met the

question in his eyes with a long, solemn stare. "Thunderhawk rides out of Two Stone Mountain in the Wind River country," she said. "I have seen him."

"Two Stone Mountain. That is new to me. Can you take me to him?" Fargo asked.

"I will show you Two Stone Mountain, nothing more," the girl said, her pretty face tightening.

"I'll take what I can get," Fargo said, and Little Flower rose effortlessly to her feet.

"I'll get my pony. I am finished here," she said.

Fargo nodded and she left the hut on quick, silent steps. He pulled himself to his feet and helped Albert to get up.

"It is good to see you, Fargo," the old scout said. "Visit again soon, before I am too old to remember the past."

"I'll try, Albert," Fargo said, and the Indian hobbled outside with him. Fargo saw Little Flower already sitting on a sturdy Indian pony with a half-brown, half-white head. He climbed onto the Ovaro, waved at Albert Twopenny, and led the way into the narrow, tree-covered passage.

Little Flower came up beside him when he was halfway through the valley and dusk had begun to slide across the land. "You are angry with me because I will not do more," she said, her jaw set.

"Am I?" Fargo returned.

"You have the right. It is for you to ask whatever you want of me," she said solemnly. "But you must find something else. Perhaps Thunderhawk is an enemy to your friends. He is a great warrior to my people."

"First, they're not my friends. Second, I don't need

explaining. I understand," he said with a trace of annoyance.

She studied him for a long moment. "Then I am glad," she said.

He spurred the Ovaro up a hillside to a half-circle of tanbark oak as night descended.

"We'll camp here. In the morning we'll pick up those who wait for me and follow you to Two Stone Mountain," he said, and little Flower slid from her pony as they reached the trees. Fargo relaxed in the darkness, decided against making a fire, and offered the girl a stick of beef jerky.

"Why do they seek Thunderhawk?" Little Flower asked as she finished the jerky and a moon rose to cast its pale light.

"It is not for me to say," he told her.

She flashed a sudden smile that hinted at wry appreciation. "You think I will chatter too much," she said.

He shrugged. "This way I won't have to wonder," he said, and she laughed—a low, warm sound.

"No wonder you and Albert Twopenny were such good friends. You are both careful as a deer," she said.

"A deer that isn't careful doesn't grow old," he answered. "Now, get some sleep. I want an early start tomorrow."

He watched as she curled up against a tree trunk and was asleep in minutes. The night stayed warm and he undressed and drew sleep around himself also.

When morning came, she woke almost when he did, and he felt her eyes on him as he rose and stretched, glancing over to where she still lay curled against the tree. He dressed unhurriedly as she watched and let her use water from his canteen to freshen up when she rose.

He set a steady pace when they began to ride, and it was late morning when he reached the North Platte, making a sharp turn to follow the river directly north. But Little Flower halted at a grassy bank, slid from the pony, and with one, quick motion, flung the deerskin dress over her head and plunged into the clear, cool water. It was done with such grace and quickness that he saw only a flash of a small, tight, coppery rear and a strong back.

She paddled in the water, dived, came up, turned, and made the exercise into a combination swim and bath. He dismounted and she stopped, only her head and shoulders above water as she peered at him. "Are you not hot with dust?" she asked.

"I wanted to make time, first," he said.

"Time is for the sun, the moon, and the wind," she said. He laughed as he took in her answer. Everything man did was meaningless rushing, she had said, and perhaps she was right, he reflected as he began to peel off his shirt.

Her eyes stayed on him as he undressed, laid his gun belt atop his clothes at the very edge of the water, and stepped into the river. The water rushed around his body, wonderfully cool and refreshing as he swam, let himself float on his back.

Little Flower swam past him, circled, came back, and then stayed demurely underwater. Finally, he swam to the shore, climbed out, and sat down on the grassy bank. He could feel the hot sun begin to dry his skin almost instantly. Little Flower watched him as she stayed in one spot treading water, and he stretched out on the grass, raising his head when he heard her come out of the water.

He lifted himself onto his elbows as she came toward him and sank down on both knees beside him. He took in the beauty of her. She was a smaller girl than she'd seemed under the deerskin dress, but she was all of a piece, everything fitting perfectly, everything balanced: sturdy legs; strong back and torso; firm, flat rear; a little belly slightly rounded; breasts just the right size, not overly large, each tipped with a pink-brown nipple on a dark-pink circle; and below the rounded belly, a small triangle with a flat, spare nap. He met her black eyes as she searched his face, glanced down over his body. Her hands reached out, touched his shoulders, moved down across his muscled chest. "You have strength of body and spirit," she remarked.

"How the hell do you know about my spirit?" Fargo said, laughing, but she did not smile as she glanced up at him.

"There are things one knows without seeing, like the wind," she said almost gravely. Her hands continued to trace a little path across his chest, pressing gently into his pectoral muscles, and he smiled inwardly. She was not beside him, showing her young, strong loveliness without reason. But the moment was not entirely calculated, he wagered silently. But he'd find that out first, he decided, and his hands reached out, cupping the two high, modest breasts. He felt their firmness, her coppery skin smooth as a rose petal, and he moved his thumbs gently over the tiny pink-brown tips.

He felt her hands tighten against his chest, then open as her palms pressed into him. But her eyes stayed on his body and she gave no other sign. He pulled gently on her breasts and she came forward, slid down on her side, and he turned her on her back.

"You are beautiful as the wild rose," he said. "You are well-named, Little Flower." Her black eyes met his, liquid inky depths that concealed more than they revealed.

He reached his lips down, took one firm, high breast and drew it into his mouth; he caressed it with his tongue and felt the brown-pink tip grow firm almost at once. He felt Little Flower's hands come up, press against his back, slide down along his spine, close over his buttocks. More than calculated, he murmured to himself, and his hands caressed her breasts as he sucked on them, then slowly moved down her body, halting at the tiny, almost flat nap, the pubic mound under it hardly covered at all. His fingers closed lower, found her dark curved places, and felt her grow moist at his touch.

Her hands moved up and down his back, and he probed into her as the sturdy, young legs fell open for him. But she made love in almost total silence, he realized. No cries, no moans, no gasped sounds of pleasure. Only soft, breathy sighs gave any sign that she felt pleasure—that, and the willing pliancy of her body, which offered itself, moved and met his every touch with silent eagerness. He felt her torso slide under him, push up to press against the throbbing warmth of his maleness as it lay hard against her.

He rose, found her waiting welcoming, and slid deeply. Her body quivered hard for an instant, and he wondered, fleetingly, if he were the first to enter the temple. She began to move her hips in rhythm with his, slowly, yet firmly, rising and falling with the sliding motions she made inside her tight warmth. And still there were only the soft, breathy sighs. Her very silence was a strangely sensual experience that made lovemaking an otherworldly experience. But her body responded, kept pace as he increased tempo, and she was wonderfully tight and warm around him. His mouth found the high, modest breasts again, and Little Flower's arms encircled his back, pulling him close to her.

He felt his pulsating desire rising, nearing its peak when, with unexpected suddenness, the soft, breathy sighs broke off and she began a low, wailing sound. It spiraled as it grew in pitch and intensity, and her young body began to quiver against him and the wailing sound grew higher, louder, a wild lostness in it and he felt the quivering outside matched by her warm, fleshed walls inside. He let himself come with her as her sturdy thighs grew tight around him and the wail reached its own climax, a sudden, sharp cry. "Jesus," he groaned as he stayed with her and the moment flooded over him with the rapture that was always too much and not enough.

The girl's sudden sharp cry broke off as quickly as it had erupted, and it became a series of almost soundless little gulps of air. He felt her belly jerk spasmodically against him until she finally grew still. He lifted his head to see her liquid orbs staring at him with dark intensity. He stayed in her until at last she moved, let him go, and he slid down beside her. She turned, pressed the high, firm breasts into his chest with unvarnished pleasure, sighed, and lay motionless until she finally lifted her head and met his gaze. He'd been more than right, he reflected as he smiled at her. But her instincts were quick—her eyes narrowed at his smile.

"You have words to say," she remarked.

"I did not ask it of you," Fargo said. "So it was not a repaying."

She met his amused gaze and he saw the flicker of a smile in the black eyes. "You know our ways too well," she said.

"Are you sorry I do?" he asked.

She looked away. "Yes," she said.

"Little Flower lies." He laughed.

She rolled away from him and sprang to her feet with a beautifully graceful motion, snatched up the deerskin dress, and pulled it over her. "I am ready to go on," she said, and the tiny smile touched her lips.

He dressed, swung onto the Ovaro, and headed north alongside the river. The afternoon had grown long when he neared Hell's Half Acre, and riding up from the south, he spotted the encampment a half-mile to the east, the horses tethered in a loose circle to one side. The men were lounging about and a small knot of figures came forward as they approached. Bertram Thorgard's jutting jaw took shape, Dallison behind him and April to the side.

Fargo brought his horse to a halt and Little Flower pulled her pony up a few yards away. He saw Thorgard glare at her at once, anger flooding his heavy face.

"Who's she?" he barked.

"Her name's Little Flower," Fargo said.

"I don't give a damn what her name is. What's she doing here with you?" Thorgard snapped.

"She's going the same way we are," Fargo said calmly, and glanced at April. The hazel-flecked eyes regarded him with cool amusement.

"I hope to hell there's more to it than that," Thorgard growled.

"There is. I found out a few things about Thunderhawk. He's a Wind River Cheyenne," Fargo said, and saw the man's eyes widen in instant interest. "Which means his home camp is somewhere in the Wind River Mountains."

Thorgard's eyes flicked to Little Flower. "She tell you that?" he questioned.

"She and an old friend," Fargo said.

"What else?" Thorgard pressed.

"She's going to show me where Thunderhawk has been seen," Fargo said.

The man's eyes stayed hard. "Then, what?" he asked.

"She goes her way," Fargo answered.

"You see to that," Thorgard snapped.

"You've got a suspicious mind," Fargo said.

Thorgard glared and stalked away, Dallison at his heels.

Fargo turned his gaze on April. "Like father, like daughter?" he asked mildly.

"I'm just an observer," she said, tossing him a quick nod as she walked slowly and sinuously away.

Fargo moved to where Little Flower sat on her pony as darkness began to roll across the land. He scanned the terrain, his eyes halting on a distant hill with a thick stand of elm trees. Behind him, a fire was lighted and he saw the men begin to line up at a sack of strips of dried beef.

"I'm hungry," Fargo said, swung from the saddle, and gestured to Little Flower. She slid from the pony and walked quietly at his side as he took his place at the end of the line with her. When he reached the sack, he pulled out a half-dozen strips of beef and warmed them over the fire on the end of a stick.

Little Flower stayed almost pressed against him and he saw her take in the men who stared at her as they ate, some with hostility, most with unconcealed desire. When he finished warming the beef, Fargo moved away and Little Flower stayed beside him as he went beyond the circle of firelight to sit down in the shadows. "Eat," he said, and handed her some of the beef. She ate hungrily, staying close to him. When she finished, she stared across at the men on the other side of the dying fire. She spoke softly but the contempt was harsh in her voice.

"They come to hunt down Thunderhawk. I laugh," she said. "He will eat them alive." Fargo's grunt was one of grim agreement as he finished his beef and rose to his feet. Little Flower rose to walk beside him to her pony.

"I don't want you to stay here," he said as the moon rose to outline the land. He pointed to the distant hill. "You sleep there, in those trees," he said.

"Will you come?" she asked.

"Yes," he said. He stepped back and she swung onto the pony and rode slowly into the night. Fargo walked back toward the fire, which now burned low, his eyes on the men as they began to bed down. He waited, watched, and saw that Thorgard stayed apart from the others under a length of canvas he suspended from two poles. Fargo scanned the campsite again and his eyes searched out April when her willowy shape stepped from the shadows to his right. She sauntered over to him, halted, and the green eyes fastened him with a long, speculative glance.

"You and she are very chummy," April slid at him.

"Just observing?" Fargo returned. She nodded as her eyes continued to search his face. "I did her a good turn. She's grateful," he said.

"I think you're about to do her another one. Or maybe you have already," April commented with a trace of tartness.

"You bothered, honey? Or just curious?" Fargo said.

"Curious," she answered.

"Curious doesn't buy you answers," Fargo said. "Come back when you're bothered."

Icicles wreathed her smile. "I won't be that bothered," she said.

"You can never tell," Fargo said cheerfully as she turned and walked away from him. He sat down and watched as she took her bedroll and put it down near Thorgard. The darkness prevented him from seeing anything more as the last of the fire went out. He stayed a little while longer, and satisfied that everyone else was still asleep, he took the Ovaro and walked to the distant hill.

Little Flower sat up as he reached the trees, and she watched him set a blanket out for himself. He undressed and she remained silent and motionless as he stretched out on the blanket. He smiled to himself as he rose up on one elbow. "I'm asking this time," he said softly.

The small figure seemed to explode in the darkness and she had the deerskin dress off before she reached the blanket and flung herself against him. Once again she made love in almost total silence, but the silence was no measure of her enjoyment, he realized as her body responded to his every act and surged with abandon against him. Her climax was again a moment of a single, sharp cry and flesh that quivered violently in pleasure. She slept curled against him afterward as though she were a kitten satisfied with food and warmth.

When morning came, she rose with him, washed, and was ready to ride before he was. Her black eyes were impassive, her face carefully composed. When he rode down to the campsite with Little Flower a few paces behind him, he saw that Thorgard had the men ready to pull out. The man's eyes went from Little Flower to Fargo with disdain, and Dallison hovered nearby.

"How long will it take us to reach the Wind River Range?" Thorgard asked.

"I'd guess we'll make it before sundown," Fargo said.

"We'll be close on your tail," Thorgard said, and turned away as April slowly rode up on a dark-gray gelding. She came up alongside the Ovaro as Little Flower walked her pony on.

"You still curious?" Fargo asked the girl.

"Yes, but about more than your choice of bedmates," April said. "You learned more than you've said."

He felt the moment of surprise at her words. "Female instincts?" he asked.

"Not entirely," she said. "But you know something you haven't said."

"I get that feeling about you, only I think you know a lot more than you've told me," he countered. "You talk and I'll talk."

She studied him and looked beautifully cool in a deep-green shirt that outlined the long curves of her breasts where it tucked tightly into the waistband of her skirt. She glanced over as Bertram Thorgard approached on his horse, the others beginning to follow. "Not now," she said quickly.

"Don't wait too long," Fargo said. He spurred the Ovaro forward and caught up to Little Flower. "Let's ride," he told her, and the girl put her pony into a fast canter to stay with him.

He held the pace with three stops during the day to rest the horses and take in fresh water. April stayed alone, he noted, resting apart from her father, and her sandy hair took on brightness in the glare of the direct sun. Thorgard and Dallison conferred off to the side at the last stop and rode together as they went on.

The afternoon had grown late when Fargo saw the Wind River Mountains rise up as they crossed the Sweetwater and drew closer to the hills. He glanced at Little Flower and pointed west along the bottom edge of the mountains. He let her lead as dusk slid down, and the land was a gray-purple when she finally reined up where a wide passage spilled down from the foothills. He followed her eyes and saw the two tall, flat stones, almost identical, facing each other some fifty yards apart, one on each side of the passage.

"Two Stone Mountain." He nodded as Thorgard rode up with Dallison. The others reined up behind and he saw April nose forward. Thorgard's glance at Little Flower was as cold as the two stones.

"She knows Thunderhawk's been seen here," Thorgard grunted.

"That's right," Fargo said.

"I'm thinking maybe she knows more than that," Dallison cut in.

Fargo's glance at Dallison was calm, but his eyes were ice-cold. "Such as?" he said carefully.

"Maybe she knows where his camp is," Dallison said.

"Maybe," Fargo said. "And maybe not. In any case, she'd not be telling us."

"She told you this much," Dallison growled.

"This much is a debt, personal. But she won't betray her own kind. It's called honor," Fargo said.

"I'm here to get my grandson back," Bertram Thorgard cut in angrily. "I don't give a shit about her sense of honor."

"Or anyone else's," April bit out.

"You mind your damn tongue." Thorgard glared at her.

Dallison's voice cut in, a sneering growl in it. "I've ways to find out what she knows," he said.

Fargo's eyes were still cold as he fastened them on the man. "You try that and I'll put a bullet between your eyes," he said.

"Don't threaten me," Dallison blustered.

"That's no threat. That's a promise," Fargo said.

"Enough," Thorgard interrupted. "Get back with the men, Frank," he ordered, and Dallison backed his horse away. Thorgard's stare was on Fargo. "The only thing that matters to me is getting my grandson back," he said. "You see what more you can get out of her before she rides out of here."

"She won't say more and I'm not asking. She's kept her part. I'll keep mine," Fargo returned.

"Goddammit, I'm paying you to find Thunderhawk, not make bargains with some squaw," Thorgard roared.

"You're paying, not owning, mister," Fargo said, and watched Thorgard's jaw muscles throb as he turned his horse away and rode back to the others. Fargo met April's green eyes as she peered at him thoughtfully.

"You're sure a hard-nose," she said. "It's almost worth the price of admission to see you stand up to him."

"You sound as if you think it's all wasted effort," he said.

"Not wasted." She shrugged. "Just remember what I told you. Nothing is ever what it seems with him."

"I'll remember," Fargo said, rode to where Little Flower sat her pony silently. "It'll be night soon," he said. "Stay and go on in the morning."

"No, not here, not with these jackals nearby. There is light enough yet. I will ride," she said, not looking at him. "And I will remember Fargo," she said, still not looking at him. She flicked a hand across the pony's neck, and the animal moved away. He watched her go on until he could no longer see her in the dusk's purple haze. But she hadn't looked back, he knew.

He turned the Ovaro, his eyes hard as he scanned the others. Thorgard had decided to make camp at one side of the wide passageway. He turned his eyes to where the horses had been tethered together on a long rope, and he peered silently at the animals, turning only when the light began to fade. The men had begun to break out blankets and settle down a dozen yards away, and Fargo pulled his horse off to the side by itself. He pulled out his own blanket, curled up on it, and sleep came almost at once. Unless he had guessed wrong, it would be a night of interrupted sleep.

He slept soundly, forced himself to stay asleep until, when the moon was high, he let himself wake. He sat up and slowly scanned the campsite. The sleeping figures were a dark mass, impossible to distinguish, and to move among them would be to risk waking a light sleeper. But he had anticipated that danger, and he rose soundlessly, creeping to where the horses were tethered. He counted quickly but carefully as he moved among them, and when he finished, he felt his lips draw back in a tight grimace. There were four horses missing. His suspicions had been all too accurate. He turned, moved away to where he'd left the Ovaro, and let the horse silently and slowly from the sleeping campsite. He climbed into the saddle only when he was certain hoofbeats wouldn't carry back to the camp. He rode along the edge of the mountain range as Little Flower had done and he knew the four riders had also done. They wouldn't have been able to pick up her trail in the darkness, but they'd have gone on for a while, halted to wait for the dawn.

Little Flower would have stopped somewhere, too. They wouldn't be all that far behind her when they spotted her trail in the new day. He swore silently as he pulled to a halt. He'd do the same with their trail, come dawn, and he dismounted, pressed himself against the base of a large elm, and catnapped. When dawn finally tinted the sky with a ragged streak of pink, he was in the saddle and he easily picked up the tracks of the four horses. The sun was still climbing over the horizon when he saw where they had stopped for the night. They weren't more than half an hour ahead of him, he estimated, and he trailed the hoof prints as they suddenly turned up into the foothills. He glimpsed the unshod pony tracks intermingled with the hoof-prints of the four riders as they pressed after Little Flower. Not expecting pursuit, she'd made no effort to mask her tracks, and Fargo swore inwardly and felt the rage churning inside him.

He slowed the Ovaro as the hoofprints veered up into a dense woods of silver fir and balsam with thick brush that grew five feet high. He saw the prints suddenly spread out and knew what that meant. They'd caught sight of Little Flower, and Fargo reined to a halt, slid from the saddle, and moved forward on foot. He heard the sound first—a sharp cry, Little Flower's voice, anger as well as pain in it. It had come from just beyond a dense thicket, and he drew the big Colt from its holster as he moved forward. Parting the heavy underbrush with his other hand, he saw Little Flower, She was stripped naked, with her arms tied behind her around the trunk of a thin sapling.

The figure in front of her had a wide belt in his hand, a heavy metal buckle swinging from one end, and Fargo saw the ugly red welt across Little Flower's abdomen.

"Start talking, squaw bitch, or I'll cut you into wolf bait," the man snarled.

The Indian girl met his snarl with icy impassiveness.

Fargo focused on the man, saw a medium-height figure, a scurvy, drawn face that seemed to wear a perpetual sneer. His glance went to the other three, who looked on with grins of enjoyment.

"Give her another one. She'll talk," one urged.

Fargo's eyes were narrowed as his thoughts raced. He didn't normally like shooting sitting ducks, but there was no choice. They were a thoroughly rotten lot, and if he tried to give them a chance to surrender, they'd come up spraying bullets. All he'd get out of it would be to lose the one advantage he had—surprise. But the three men looking on were spread out in a half-circle, too far apart to bring them all down in one burst of fire. Fargo dropped into a crouch just as he saw the one with the belt bring his arm up to lash out again.

"You want to do it the hard way, girlie," the man rasped as he started to strike out.

Fargo's finger pressed the trigger of the Colt and

the shot resounded as though it were a cannon's roar in the little thicket. The belt flew into the air as the man spun in a half-circle before falling, a gush of red spurting from his shattered ribs. The other three whirled, started to draw their guns, but Fargo had the Colt shifted instantly and he fired off two more shots. Two of the men toppled as though they were ten-pins in a bowling alley. As he fired the last of the two shots, Fargo flung himself down and forward and hit the ground as the third figure sent a hail of bullets smashing through the thin branches over his head. Fargo fired from the ground where he lay on his stomach, two more shots. The man flew backward, almost doubled in two as a crimson spray showered the nearby green foliage.

The four figures lay lifeless in the thicket, and Fargo pushed himself to his feet. The echoes of the brief and savage burst of gunfire died away and silence enveloped the woods at once, as though nature were eager to blanket this interruption of her domain. Fargo stepped to the thin sapling and untied Little Flower. She leaned against him and seemed suddenly very small.

"You're all right, now," he told her, and she nodded, stepped back, and picked the deerskin dress from the grass. She drew it on with quiet dignity, and her glance moved across the figures on the ground, returned to Fargo, her face grave.

"Four less for Thunderhawk to kill," she said.

"Yes," Fargo agreed.

"And one more thing to make me remember Fargo," she said.

"Good." He smiled. "I might come visiting Albert

again sometime. Now go back to your people. I've some unfinished business."

She nodded, unsmiling, climbed onto the pony, and the thick woods quickly swallowed her from sight. But once again he was certain she hadn't looked back, and he smiled as he walked to where he'd left the Ovaro. He had begun to understand her. The discipline of the spirit was as important as the discipline of the body.

He climbed onto the pinto and began to retrace his steps, feeling his jaw grow tight almost at once. He was certain about one thing: the four men hadn't acted on their own. The cold anger hardened inside him with every mile he rode. When he finally reached the campsite, the sun was in the midafternoon sky, and his lake-blue eyes were cold. He rode into the camp and his hand rested on the butt of the big Colt at his side. He saw Thorgard under the canvas top, April on the ground nearby, using her saddle as a back rest. He rode closer, his eyes searching the small, scattered groups of figures that dotted the ground, and he reined to a halt as he spotted Dallison, seeing the man quickly jump to his feet.

Fargo swung from the saddle, stepped away from the horse, and saw three men quickly back away from where Dallison faced him. "You son of a bitch," Fargo said.

Alarm pushed the surprise from Dallison's slitted eyes.

"Fargo, you hold on now," he heard Thorgard call out, and saw the man come from under the canvas top out of the corner of his eye. "*Fargo!*" Thorgard called again, more sharply, this time. But Fargo's gaze bored into Dallison, the icy message unmistakable.

Dallison stayed motionless, arms at his sides, for a long moment, and Fargo wondered if he'd misjudged the man. Maybe fear had given him a sudden dose of common sense. But he saw the almost imperceptible twitch of Dallison's hand and smiled inwardly. He hadn't misjudged the man. Dallison was too stupid and too small to have much common sense. He watched as Dallison's hand yanked at his gun, a rough, jerking motion that destroyed whatever speed it had. Fargo let him get his six-gun almost clear of its holster before he drew the Colt with a motion as smooth and fast as a diamondback's strike.

The Colt fired while Dallison was still bringing his six-gun up, and Fargo caught the last flash of surprise in the slitted eyes as the heavy slug slammed through him. Dallison staggered back as the gun fell from his hand. He swayed, half-turned as legs, robbed of the strength of life, collapsed under him and he sank down to become a motionless heap.

"Goddamn you, Fargo. I need every man I have," Thorgard thundered.

Fargo still held the Colt in his hand as he turned to Bertram Thorgard. "Now you've got five less," he said evenly. "Were you in on this with Dallison?"

"No, it was all his idea. I didn't know about it till I woke up this morning and found you gone. I figured you went after them," Thorgard said.

Fargo's eyes bored into the man, but Bertram Thorgard's heavy face revealed nothing. "I guess I'm never going to know if you're lying," Fargo said. "Which is goddamn lucky for you."

Thorgard allowed no reaction to these words to show in his face. "What's done is done," he said. "You just forget what you know or don't know and start finding that Cheyenne camp."

Fargo holstered the Colt, his eyes still hard. "We can get in a few hours' riding before dark. We'll head up into the mountains," he said.

Thorgard turned to bark at the men nearby. "Mount up. Two of you stay here and bury Dallison. You can catch up to us when you're finished. Time's important," he said.

Fargo saw April start to saddle the dark-gray gelding, and he led the Ovaro over to her as Thorgard pulled his canvas down. "I keep thinking of what you said, nothing is ever as it seems with him," Fargo commented. "Got any opinions?"

"No opinions," April said as she tightened the cinch under the horse. "But I can tell you one thing. He knew damn well you could outshoot Dallison."

Fargo nodded as he climbed onto the Ovaro and rode slowly away. Her words danced through his mind as their cryptic meaning grew clear. She had told him nothing and everything, he realized. It was unlikely Dallison had sent the four men out on his own, he realized, and April's words had put it all into place. Thorgard had heard what he'd promised Dallison if Little Flower were harmed. He'd heard it and yet he let Dallison send the men out. April had spelled out the answer in her own oblique way. Thorgard had been willing to sacrifice Dallison for hard information about Thunderhawk's camp. He'd taken a calculated risk.

Fargo let a harsh sound escape his lips. It had been a calculated risk that had failed. Thorgard had gotten nothing and lost five men, and Fargo took some satisfaction in that. But once again he realized that it would be a dangerous mistake to underestimate the depths of Bertram Thorgard's duplicity. Only duplicity might be the wrong word. There was something else driving the man—something dark and twisted that April's words had only hinted at. But she knew her father, perhaps better than she wanted to, Fargo mused. More and more, April was becoming the key to a lot of things. Maybe staying alive was one of them.

He had to get her to talk, but that would take some careful doing, he knew. She was her own kind of cactus. She was too bright to be smooth-talked and maybe too principled to be lightly swayed. But there was fear churning inside her, beneath her controlled exterior. He had to find a way to make it break loose. He shook his head, pushing away further speculation as he searched the low hills for a place to camp, finally finding a high ravine long enough to accommodate everyone.

Fargo ate quickly as night fell, the tiredness flooding his body as he took down his bedroll and slept quickly in the warm night, his plans for the morning already set.

4

"I don't like it one damn bit," Bertram Thorgard snapped in the bright sun of the new day.

"I didn't figure you would," Fargo said.

"Dammit, we ought to be staying close to you," Thorgard said.

"There's no way I'm going to find Thunderhawk's camp, much less get near it, with that herd following along," Fargo said.

"My plans to take the boy call for every one of these men," Thorgard protested.

"After I find Thunderhawk," Fargo reminded him.

"You expect me to sit around here and just wait for you to get back to me?" The man frowned.

"No, you and your crew ride, stay together, and keep heading north. The Cheyenne will be watching, you can be damn sure of that. They'll watch, wait, and wonder what the hell you're doing up here. It'll keep some of them busy for a while," Fargo said.

"When do I hear from you?" Thorgard queried.

"When I've something to tell you," Fargo said. "I want one rider with me, to send back if I need to."

"Pick one," Thorgard said.

"April," Fargo said calmly, and saw Thorgard's face darken instantly.

"No, absolutely not," the man snapped.

"I wouldn't ride with one of those jackals behind me," Fargo said. "I'll take April."

"I said no," Thorgard thundered. "I can't risk it. I need her when I take the boy."

"You don't need her now, and now comes first. I don't find Thunderhawk, you don't get the boy." He saw the man's mouth twitch as Thorgard wrestled with himself. "April," Fargo said calmly.

Thorgard spun, gestured to April, and she followed him as he stalked a dozen yards away, far enough to be out of earshot. He turned to April and Fargo saw him gesticulate angrily, his face dark with inner tension. Thorgard struggled to keep his voice low, but it flared up for a moment in tense anger. "I don't care what you think, dammit," Fargo heard Thorgard rasp, and then instantly bring his voice down again. The largely one-sided conversation went on for another few minutes until Thorgard finally broke it off.

Fargo waited by the Ovaro as the man strode back to him. April followed, her high-cheekboned face drawn in tightly.

Thorgard halted in front of him. "All right, she'll ride with you," the man said. "But I need her for the boy. You better not stick her neck in a noose."

"Hell, you beat me to that, Thorgard," Fargo returned, and swung onto the pinto as the man's face reddened. He moved the horse on as Thorgard strode away, waiting while April climbed onto the dark-gray gelding and came up beside him.

He headed the Ovaro up the wide passageway into the mountains and she rode with him in silence, her longish breasts swaying gently under a pale-tan blouse. She rode well, he noted, her long back held straight, her body in tune with the horse.

"Get your traveling orders straight?" he slid at her.

"Orders. Reminders. Threats. All the same," she murmured, and the bitterness was in her voice again.

"You changed your mind about talking?" Fargo asked.

"No, but there were things I never planned to talk about and I don't now," April said.

"We'll see," Fargo remarked. "Plans change."

She said nothing and turned the horse into a narrow pass that appeared to the right. It led sharply upward and he rode on ahead. He waited for her on a flat ridge when she emerged from the pass. His eyes swept the terrain, but nothing moved except a covey of ruffed grouse and he rode on. The terrain was lush, thick with foliage, good green mountain country with plenty of elk, bear, and deer. He spotted unshod pony tracks that crossed one another and faded away, saw a wrist gauntlet where a party of braves had camped down and continued on in a slow circle. He followed a trail of prints through a leafy arbor and lost them where a wide bed of white cushion moss fanned out so deep its spongy surface had sprung back to obliterate the trail.

He halted at a mountain stream to refresh and rest the horses and watched as April knelt down, her long, willowy form bending gracefully as she pressed the cool water into her face with both hands.

"You ready to talk some?" Fargo asked.

She looked up at him and wiped her face dry. "You first. You held back something you learned. Why?" she asked.

"Didn't feel it'd really matter much," he said.

"Try me?" April said.

"Thunderhawk made your sister one of his wives," Fargo said, and April's face remained expressionless as she listened. "She died a few years after," he finished.

April stared into space for a moment. "Why did you think it wouldn't matter?" she asked.

"Your pa never mentions her. He talks only about the boy, taking the boy back, getting him home safe. It's as if she never existed. I figured he probably thought she was killed in the attack. Knowing Thunderhawk kept her for a few years wouldn't matter any now, especially since she's died, anyway."

"You're right. It won't matter to him," April said, bitterness filling her voice with a sudden rush. "There's no need to talk of it."

"What about you? Does it matter to you?" Fargo questioned.

"It matters, but not the way it would have once," April answered, and a tiny furrow came between her eyebrows. "I told you I haven't been with him for ten years. I was the older sister and I was sent to an aunt—banished, if you prefer," April said.

"Why?" Fargo questioned.

"He couldn't break me. I became too much trouble for him," April said. "Aunt Tessie raised me as a daughter and she was confined to a wheelchair. We helped each other, and I'll always be grateful to her."

"And Mary?" Fargo pressed.

"He kept her with him. She was his favorite," April said.

"Then he can care about someone," Fargo offered, and drew a quick and angry glance.

"Care? His idea of care is owning. It means doing what he wants, when he wants, and how he wants. It means obeying his every whim, being the butt of his rages, being totally smothered until you hate waking up in the morning."

"Is that what happened to your sister?" Fargo asked.

"Yes," April said sharply, the word tearing out of her.

"But you didn't do anything for her," he said.

"I couldn't," April flung back. "I couldn't. I seldom even got to see her. But she wrote me, long letters that told me what life was like with him. I cried for her, God, did I cry for her. Maybe because I was helpless to do anything about it."

"He's got some hold on you. That's why you're here. What is it?" Fargo asked.

"It doesn't matter. I'm here," April said darkly.

"There's something you haven't told me, something more to all of it," Fargo said.

"I didn't say that," April protested quickly.

"No, but it's in the things you don't say. You say words that cast shadows behind them," he told her.

"I've said all I'm going to say, maybe too much," April told him, and her chin lifted firmly.

"Or not enough," he said, and saw her lips grow tight. "Let's ride," he said, and climbed onto the pinto. He'd back off for now, he decided silently. Pressing wouldn't work with her. He had to lead her to it, like a skittish filly on guard against the real and the imagined. If there was time, he added grimly, and set his mind to exploring another set of tracks he spotted. They faded away as the night descended and he halted beneath two huge cottonwoods that offered safety and seclusion.

April had beef jerky in her saddlebag and shared it with him as she stretched out on the ground under the moon's pale glow, all long, flowing curves. When they finished eating, she rose, and went to her saddlebag, and pulled out a dark-blue robe. She turned and saw him watching her.

"We're not all children of nature," she said, and he heard the tartness in her voice. "I'm sure you're disappointed in that," she added.

"I am," he said.

"Disappointment is good for the character. It builds self-discipline," she said, taking the robe and disappearing into the trees.

He undressed to his underwear bottoms, spread out his bedroll, and lay down on it on one elbow.

When April returned, the dark-blue robe was wrapped tightly around her long figure. She paused to gaze at his muscled hardness in the pale moonlight and the quietly amused smile edged her lips. "Are you trying to excite me, Fargo?" she asked, laughter in her voice.

"Wouldn't think of it," he said.

"The hell you wouldn't," she returned as she lay down and pulled the blanket around her.

"You're just being curious again," he commented.

"And curiosity doesn't buy me answers, you said," she tossed back.

"But enough of it might buy you something else," he said, and laughed.

"I'll try to remember that." She turned her back to him.

He stretched out and went to sleep as the night grew still. Fargo woke twice, once at a cougar's cry and once at the sound of moose nearby. Morning came, hot and bright, and he rose first, glancing across at April. She had turned in her sleep and the top of the robe had come open enough for him to see the two long, smooth curves as they swelled to fullness. He was still gazing at her when she woke, snapped her eyes open, and pulled the neck of the robe closed as she sat up. Her frown was instantaneous as she focused still-sleep-filled eyes on him. He laughed as he donned trousers and gun belt, went into the forest, and finally returned with two handfuls of wild pears.

She was dressed, the pale-tan blouse resting lightly on the full bottoms of her breasts as she tucked the ends of the garment into her skirt.

"We ride slow and quiet," he told her, and she nodded and finished the last of the pears. With April close behind him, he set a circular path that picked up numerous sets of unshod prints, but all faded away in time. The thick mountain woodland offered both concealment and difficulty as it allowed few easy trails to pick up in its leaf-covered terrain. He climbed slowly as he circled, stayed with the search, his eyes ceaselessly sweeping the land around them in all directions.

April picked up the silent tension that was part of the endless caution and painstaking pursuit. As the day finally began to wind down and he halted in a glen to let the horses graze on sweetfern, she gave a deep sigh. "I'm tired," she breathed. "I know I haven't seen a fraction of the things you have, but I'm exhausted from looking."

"Just a little farther, to the end of the next hillside," he said, and moved the Ovaro forward again.

She came up beside him as the hillside ended and began its descent on the other side of a rounded, heavily treed crest, and halted beside him as he reined up. Through the trees, in the dim distance, the Indian camp was visible, four tepees plainly in sight.

"Maybe that's it," April whispered, excitement in her quick intake of breath.

"Relax. That's only a hunting camp," Fargo said.

"But maybe they'll lead us to the main camp," she said.

"Wrong Indians," Fargo grunted, and she frowned, straining her eyes to peer through the trees.

"How can you tell at this distance? I can hardly see them," April said, frowning.

"I can see the tepees," Fargo said. "Four poles. The Cheyenne use a three-pole tepee." He backed the pinto and turned the horse west into higher land.

April cast a sidelong glance at him. 'You keep impressing me," she said.

"I can do better." Fargo grinned and drew a cool smile.

"Obviously not with your modesty," April returned.

He chuckled and spurred the pinto on to a small glen circled by tall, fragrant balsams. He halted, swung to the ground, and tethered the horses inside the trees, returning with his bedroll.

April undressed inside the tree cover and, wrapped in the dark-blue robe, went to sleep almost the instant she stretched out.

He lay awake a little longer and thought about how to pry more information out of her. Coming up with no answers, he pushed aside his idle musings and slept until morning.

He rose while April still slept, and he saw the little glen nestled at the edge of ridge of land that looked out over a series of valleys and hillsides, plateaus, and tree-covered ravines. The Wind River Mountains were lush, thick with green beauty, and he let his eyes move slowly across every foot of the terrain, reading the land the way other men read books. Leaves became an alphabet, sentences formed passages, the very ground a poem where nature wrote the verses. He heard April come up behind him and saw that she had dressed, changing the pale-tan blouse for a pale-green one that deepened the green of her eyes.

She surveyed the mountains and valleys beside him and shrugged. "Which way? Or do we toss a coin?"

"No coin. We go west, down that ravine," Fargo said, and April frowned at him.

"Why? What do you see that has you go that way. I don't see a damn thing to make me pick one way over another," she said.

"That's because we look with different eyes," Fargo said.

"Let me look with your eyes. Please," April said.

He paused, turning back to the hillsides that stretched before them. "The hills and woods are honeycombed with trails. Most in front of us are elk trails, moose and deer paths. These trails have their own character. Tree bark is worn on both sides of the trail as the herds pass through. The ground becomes grooved, worn down so only nut moss can get a foothold to grow. The trails there in the west are used by horses and riders. No bark worn from the trees, grass covers the ground, the trails curve back and forth. Deer and elk trains are pretty much straight. They also go up and down hill. Man-made trails cut across country, wind, and backtrack," Fargo told her.

"Amazing," she said. "But the trails could be made by any number of Cheyenne. It still seems like looking for a needle in a haystack."

"Not really. You eliminate some things and concentrate on others," Fargo said.

"What do you eliminate?" April asked.

"All the steep mountain areas. You can't put a main camp on them. Same for all the craggy places and high ridges. You pass up all the high plateau areas, too. They're too open for a Cheyenne base camp."

"What's left to concentrate on?"

"Forested areas where they can cut down enough trees and still stay hidden away. And one thing more, very important: water," Fargo said. "A hunting camp, trail camp, war camp, they can all be anywhere. But a main camp will always be by water, a lake or a good-sized mountain stream. You put the important things together and you don't waste time looking in wrong places."

"I'm impressed, Fargo. Again," April said as she walked back to the horses beside him.

"You have to know what to look for before you know what to do," Fargo remarked blandly as he swung onto the Ovaro.

"Do you always know what to look for?" she slid at him, the cool smile toying with her lips.

"Always have," he said.

"Never made a mistake?" she returned.

"Maybe." He laughed and sent the pinto down a steep slope. He rode steadily, his eyes sweeping the mountains.

The day had begun to wind toward an end when he reined up, put a finger to his lips, and April slowly came to join him. She followed his gaze as he stared down at a path below where the leaves moved in a snakelike thread. As the foliage thinned, the line of almost-naked riders came into sight, traveling single-file, the last one dragging a slain deer behind his pony.

"Cheyenne," Fargo murmured as he counted six braves.

He stayed on the ground, riding parallel to the path of the riders below until he saw them enter a flat, forested area. He nodded to April to follow and sent the Ovaro carefully downward to swing behind the Cheyenne. He stayed far back and watched the riders move through a thick forest of balsam and fir that began to thin out. He reined up, slid from his horse, and April swung from the gray gelding.

He left the horses tethered to a low branch and moved forward on foot, halted, and glanced at April as the unmistakable sound of swift-running water drifted to them. She nodded and he went forward where the land began to slope downward. He halted, dropped to one knee as the camp came into sight between the trees. The six riders entered the camp and Fargo risked moving half a dozen yards closer, halting as his eyes surveyed the camp.

A large irregularly shaped oblong, the camp backed up onto a wide, fast-running mountain stream that flowed by the entire length of the camp at the far side. He saw all the fixtures he'd expected to find in a main camp—meat-drying racks, piles of hot stones by a small fire, hide and skinning areas where three old squaws worked on two elk hides stretched out flat.

The squaw tepees were off to one side, he noted, and at the far end of the camp, a large tepee stood apart from all the others, its hide walls the only ones decorated with sticklike figures and drawings that were both childish yet very adult. "Thunderhawk's tepee," he muttered to April, and swept the camp again with a slow glance.

His quick count told him there were some fifty braves in the camp. He guessed there'd be another twenty-five out hunting and scouting through the mountains. Bertram Thorgard would need every one of the men he'd brought as arrow fodder.

Fargo's eyes followed some dozen children scattered about the camp. "You see the boy?" he asked, his voice a low whisper.

"I won't know him any more than you will," she answered. "But all of these children look too old or too young."

Fargo nodded in agreement and let his eyes sweep the camp again as his mind took note of trees, rocks, shapes, the position of tepees, and the way one border of the camp was actually a swift-running stream. He caught sight of a movement at the large tepee and was staring at it when the flap pulled back and a man stepped out. His identity was apparent in his commanding presence as he surveyed the camp with the powerful head of an eagle, his eyes black as live coals.

"Thunderhawk," Fargo murmured.

April's eyes fixed on the Cheyenne chief. "He's a handsome man," she breathed, and Fargo nodded. He took in the man's powerful body, naked except for a loincloth, broad, well-muscled shoulders, chest high and wide, and legs not unlike a bronze statue. The Cheyenne were taller than most tribes, and Thunderhawk was a tall Cheyenne. His height only added to the handsome imperiousness with which he surveyed the camp. But this was no superficial mask, Fargo realized as he studied the man's strong, chiseled face. Every powerful plane emphasized determination, intelligence, and perhaps most dangerous of all, the tenacity and wisdom of the undefeated.

"Daddy better have that hole card you say he always has," Fargo grunted.

"He will," April said. "He will."

Fargo's eyes were still on Thunderhawk when he saw the man reach back to pull the flap open. The boy came out of the tepee, black-eyed, his near-naked body thoroughly tanned, his hair a sandy brown. Fargo felt April's hand tighten on his arm.

"That's him. That has to be him. He's the only one that fits," April breathed.

"You're right," Fargo agreed.

"A handsome child," April murmured almost as if to herself.

"He's not running with the other kids. Thunderhawk has made him special. He stays in the chief's tepee. He's being treated as a prize captive," Fargo said.

April glanced at him, her eyes sharp. "Why?"

"Could be a lot of reasons. Some tribes sell prize captives for a lot of money. He could be keeping the boy safe and guarded until he's old enough to bring a handsome price," Fargo said. "Or maybe it's just personal with him. He did make your sister one of his wives. Maybe the boy's a special kind of possession, like his favorite bear-claw necklace."

April's lips were pressed together tightly as she stared at Thunderhawk and the boy. "Do you see any way to get the boy out?" she asked.

"First, you'll have to bring your getaway horses down beyond the end of the camp. Then, if you could get the boy without being seen, you'd have to make a run for it down the stream."

"That's a large *if*, isn't it?" she said.

"Large as a damn mountain," Fargo growled.

"What now?" April asked.

"We've found the camp and the boy. We go tell your pa. It'll be dark in an hour. We'll ride by night. If he kept north, as I told him to do, we ought to find him by dawn," Fargo said.

He rose and started back to the horses with April at his side. He sank to the ground when they reached the horses, leaning back against a tree. "We'll catnap," he said.

She slid down against a tree of her own and closed her eyes and he saw her find sleep quickly. He pulled slumber around himself and let the night descend. The moon was high when he woke, his body rested. April came awake at his touch and silently followed as he led the way from the mountain slope.

They rode most of the night with two stops to nap, and when dawn came, Fargo saw that Thorgard had followed his orders as he spotted the body of men still asleep in a long dip in the land. Thorgard woke when they rode in, and the man's excitement was almost palpable. "I've told the men exactly what they're to do, laid out the plan perfectly," Thorgard said as he rubbed his hands in anticipation. "We'll fake an attack. Thunderhawk will come at us full force, of course, figuring he has all the advantages. But the men will give ground as they fire back, let him come after us, draw him out farther and farther. Then, when we've drawn him out far enough, we dig in and fight, keep him real busy. While all that is going on, we take the boy."

"Thunderhawk won't empty the camp. Getting the boy out may be impossible," Fargo said. "It'll be like sticking your head into a hornet's nest."

"I know you can do it, Fargo, with April along to take care of the boy," Thorgard said, and Fargo felt the frown dig into his brow as he stared at the man.

"What do you mean, I can do it?" he shot back. "I agreed to find Thunderhawk for you, nothing else. That was the deal."

Bertram Thorgard's face darkened instantly. "Getting the boy was the deal," he snapped.

"Bullshit," Fargo answered. "You made your own crazy plans for that. I wasn't in on them. I found Thunderhawk for you. I've done my job."

Thorgard met his angry eyes and Fargo watched the man's lips purse slowly. "Maybe you have," Thorgard said with unexpected reasonableness. "I always like to be fair." Fargo felt surprise stab at him. "I'll have one of the men go in with April," Thorgard said calmly.

"What?" Fargo blurted. "None of those drifters you hired has a snowball in hell's chance of pulling it off."

"One of them will have to do it," Thorgard said.

"Why not shoot him now? April, too. Save the Cheyenne the trouble," Fargo spat out.

"I'm here to get the boy. I'm not changing my plans. One of the men will go in with April," Thorgard said, and his small shrug was a suddenly helpless gesture. "I've no choice. You've pulled out," he said.

Fargo's lake-blue eyes bored into the man and he felt rage churning inside himself. "You bastard," Fargo hissed. "You rotten bastard. You counted on this all along, didn't you?"

"I don't know what you're talking about, Fargo," Thorgard protested mildly.

"Hell, you don't," Fargo threw back. "You know I'd see that none of those drifters has a chance of getting the boy out. You figured I couldn't stand by and let you send April to her death with him."

Thorgard's face remained expressionless as he shrugged. "Don't go. Prove me wrong," he said, unable to keep the edge of triumph from his voice.

"Goddamn you, I can't, and you know why," Fargo roared.

"Because you know I'll go through with it my way," Thorgard said almost chidingly.

"Yes, damn you, that's exactly what I know," Fargo cursed.

Bertram Thorgard's face grew suddenly harsh. "Enough talk. You going to take her in to get the boy or not?" he barked.

"You son of a bitch. When this is over, if you're still alive, I'll do some settling with you," Fargo promised darkly, and felt the fury of frustration. The man's face held an icy smugness. "I estimate we'll reach the camp in four hours. You start back ahead of us. That'll give you time to be in position when we mount our attack," Thorgard said. "Now, where do we meet you afterward?"

Fargo thought for a moment. "The stream that runs along the back of the camp goes all the way down the mountainside. It makes a sharp curve where it reaches a small valley. I'll meet you there," Fargo said.

"I'll find it. Now, I'll go over plans with the men once more," Thorgard said, and strode away. Fargo turned, feeling April's hand on his arm. He saw that the green eyes were filled with a terrible weariness.

"You don't have to do this. I'll understand," she said.

"But then I'll have to avoid looking in mirrors the rest of my life," Fargo answered.

"And so he wins again, as always," April said, and Fargo heard the bitter anger in her voice. "I almost wish you wouldn't go, just to see him lose for once."

"You did say *almost*, didn't you?" Fargo grinned.

"Yes, I did say *almost*." April nodded. "I'm not noble enough for anything else."

"Let's ride. It won't get any easier standing here," Fargo said, and turned the Ovaro north.

5

Fargo lay flat on his belly in the tall underbrush, April close beside him. A half-dozen yards away, the stream coursed swiftly along the edge of the Cheyenne camp. They had ridden hard and he had set a path that brought them to the camp's back side. They'd left the horses far downstream and stayed on foot in the heavy brush until they came in sight of the camp. They had crawled from there, staying well-hidden in the tall, thick brush as Fargo studied the lay of the camp again. Finally, he pushed back and turned to April. "Now we wait," he said.

"And maybe pray some?" she offered.

"Anything you think will help," he agreed.

April's hand reached out, coming to rest on his arm. "I know that if I make it through this alive it'll be because of you," she said. "Thank you seem such weak words for that."

"Words are like clothes. Sometimes we have to do with the only ones we've got," he said.

April's hand stayed on his arm and she leaned

toward him, her lips opening, and he felt their warm sweetness against his mouth. There was tenderness and a hint of something more in the soft pressure that lingered.

"When words aren't enough," she murmured as she pulled away.

"Careful." He smiled. "I might come around for more when this is over."

"I might just be there," she said, and turned on her side. He watched as she stared into the distance, her hazel-flecked eyes growing dark as a tightness touched the finely edged lips.

"What are you thinking?" he asked.

"That I'm here, you're here, and he always wins and I hate him," April said.

"Hating's for later. Finding a way to get out of here alive is for now," Fargo said, and turned onto his stomach, scanning the big camp with another slow, careful sweep. Thunderhawk came into view, the boy at his side, and the Indian chief beckoned to a toothless old squaw who hurried forward at once. His voice carried clearly across the stream and to the underbrush where Fargo lay beside April.

"Let the boy watch as you make moccasins, old woman," Thunderhawk said. "Let him learn."

The old squaw nodded and took the boy with her as she stepped into a nearby tepee. Fargo saw another, equally old squaw follow the first one into the tent, and he watched as Thunderhawk walked to where a number of his braves were feathering new arrow shafts. The Cheyenne chief passed among them, examining each shaft with a critical eye. At his nod, the warriors beamed proudly. It was plain they admired their chief's wisdom and leadership. Thunderhawk had just finished inspecting the workmanship of his men when the three riders raced into the camp at full speed.

Fargo spoke more than enough Siouan to understand their shouts, but even if he hadn't, their excited message was clear. Thorgard and his men had been spotted on their way, and as Fargo watched, Thunderhawk barked crisp orders. He conveyed a sense of firm control, Fargo saw, allowing no wild and wasteful excitement. At another command, his braves leapt onto their ponies with quiet precision as Thunderhawk watched, his handsome face and coal-fire eyes exuding disciplined strength. He turned and swung onto a brown horse.

With a quick, chopping motion of one arm, Thunderhawk sent his warriors out of the camp at a full gallop. The quiet discipline would vanish with the attack, Fargo knew. The Cheyenne would erupt into a wild ferocity, concerned only with destroying the enemy. Rage would become another kind of discipline that only Thunderhawk could control because, as Chief of the Wind River Cheyenne, he understood that wedding of fury and order that made the superior warrior.

As the sound of the racing riders faded away, Fargo returned his gaze to the camp. As he'd expected, Thunderhawk had not taken all his braves from the camp, and April's whisper followed his gaze. "I count ten braves left," she said.

"You missed two at the far end and three more back by the birches. That makes fifteen," Fargo said. "And some thirty squaws. Don't underestimate the squaws," he added as he caught April's quick glance. "They can be vicious as bobcats."

"How do we get into that tepee without being seen?" April asked.

"We know there are at least two squaws in there, maybe more," Fargo said. "That means I can't cut my way in through the back,"

"Two old crones," April dismissed them.

"Old crones shout," Fargo said sharply. "So do little boys. One alarm from anybody and we've had it for sure. I'm going to have to be quick and final. There's no room for anything less. I'm going to try to slip in through the front and cut my way out through the back." April nodded and he gestured downstream. "When I start, you move down until you're positioned in back of it but on this side of the stream. You wait there for my signal," he said.

She nodded and he turned from her, scanning the camp again.

The tepee with the boy inside was set back from the stream, perhaps a yard or two, he estimated. Most of the braves had gathered in a knot in the center of the camp. The younger squaws continued their work at the hides and meat-drying racks. Fargo cast a glance at April and crawled forward into the cold water of the swift-running stream. He stayed on his belly, letting the water flow over him, and raising his head only enough to gulp in air.

When he reached the other bank, he crawled half out of the water and felt naked in the open flatness of the soft ground. He inched his way toward the tepee, pressing himself as flat as he could. He knew that if anyone glanced directly over at the stream near the tepee they'd see him, and he forced himself to continue to crawl, staying down as he inched his way forward. A wide patch of dropseed grass rose up to his left, and he was grateful for its few inches of protection. He neared the front of the tepee, halted, keeping his face pressed to the ground as he peered across the camp. Everyone was still busy with their own tasks. He hadn't been spotted. He'd stretched the boundaries of luck and was properly grateful.

He inched the last few feet to the tent flap, drew a kerchief from his back pocket, and stuffed it inside his belt where he could reach it more quickly. The bottom of the tent flap hung loosely, and he lifted it with one hand, slid himself halfway under it and paused. The interior of the tepee was lighted by a fire in a pit at one side. The toothless old squaw sat near the fire, and he saw a partially completed moccasin of buffalo hide in front of her. She was cutting an ankle flap for it out of another piece of hide. The boy watched from almost beside her and both had their backs to the entrance to the tepee. Fargo took in the second squaw. She was closer, sitting cross-legged as she bound pieces of stone chips onto the ends of hide-scraper handles. He saw that she had three finished scrapers on the ground at her feet as he pulled his long legs into the tepee.

She was only a few feet away now, and Fargo rose slowly into a crouch, took two long steps on feet silent as a cougar's prowl, and closed his hand around the old squaw's scrawny neck. He saw her eyes bulge as he tightened his grip and held it. In seconds, she passed into unconsciousness. He let her slide to her side and looked up at the other old squaw. The woman was intent on her work, her aged ears no longer sharp, but he saw the boy turn to stare at him. The boy sat galvanized for a second and then pushed the old squaw with his hand. The woman turned, saw Fargo, and her ancient eyes grew wider, a frown adding to the wrinkles in her face. Her mouth dropped open to scream, but Fargo had scooped up one of the hide scrapers. He flung it in a short, accurate line, and the tool plowed into the old crone's forehead. It stuck there not unlike a grotesque monument as the old squaw toppled over.

Fargo darted forward as the boy started to streak for the tent flap. Cutting the small form off and seizing one arm, he spun the boy around, yanked the kerchief from his waist, and stuffed it into the boy's mouth before he could cry out. With one, quick motion he had the gag in place and tied. He drew the doubled-edged throwing knife from its calf holster around his leg, and carrying the boy under one arm, he sliced the knife down the back of the tepee. He cut swiftly, a slit long enough for him to step through. Fargo felt the boy try to wriggle free; he squeezed hard with his arm and the boy stopped struggling.

Half out of the tepee, Fargo glanced to his right, saw no one at the stream, and waved one arm furiously at the high brush on the other side of the water. April appeared at once, coming toward him across the stream. She hurried, but she took care not to splash, he noticed. When she reached him, he handed her the boy, drew the big Colt, and glanced around once more before stepping into the stream. "This way," he whispered as he started down the center of the stream in a long, loping crouch.

Carrying the boy against her, April followed at his heels, and the stream curved and ran through a deep forest, bubbling onward through the trees. They had gone perhaps a hundred yards, Fargo guessed, when he heard the scream, a squaw's voice, quickly followed by deeper shouts.

"Somebody went into the tepee," he said to April. He saw the fear instantly flood her face.

"They'll be coming after us," she breathed.

"Not that fast," he said, and saw her questioning frown. "They'll search for tracks on the other side first. When they don't find any, they'll know the boy was taken by the stream—but they still won't know which way. They'll have to go up- or downstream or send a search party each way. All that'll take time. We'll have plenty of distance on them by then." He reached back and she gave him the boy. He caught the glare in the boy's black eyes as he tossed the small form over his shoulder.

Fargo increased speed, letting the water splash noisily now as he continued downstream until he reached the place where they'd left the horses. He put the boy in the saddle in front of him and rode the Ovaro back into the stream. April followed on her gray and Fargo slowed the pinto as the terrain dropped off and the stream sloped downward sharply. He let the horse find its own footing and resumed a fast trot only after the stream leveled off again. He rode steadily, staying in the stream as it wandered back and forth down the mountains. He saw the strain in April's face and slowed, halted the horses in the middle of the stream.

"They're not coming after us," Fargo said. "We'd have heard them by now."

"Why not?" April frowned.

"I'd guess they realized they'd lost too much time

looking and decided to wait for Thunderhawk to return and make the decisions," Fargo said.

"He'll come," April said, and he was surprised at the grimness in her voice.

"You always such a pessimist?" he asked.

"Maybe," she said.

Fargo's lips pursed in thought. "I think you're right in this instance. He'll have a try at recapturing the boy, no Cheyenne chief will give up a prize captive easily."

"I'm ready to go on," April said.

Fargo reached around and took the kerchief from the boy's mouth. The small form spun in the saddle to spear him with the fury in his eyes. The boy's fist came up in an attempt to smash it into Fargo's face, and the Trailsman deflected the blow with his palm. His voice was harsh as he spoke to the boy in Siouan.

"Be careful or I'll leave you for the wolves," he growled.

The boy's lips curled at him, but he lowered his arm and turned in the saddle.

"He hates us," April said.

"It's common enough with many children retaken. He's spent more years as a Cheyenne than he has a white boy," Fargo said. "He'll have to be brought around slowly."

"You mean recivilized," April said.

"Your word, not mine," he snapped, and sent the Ovaro on through the stream. He halted after another quarter of a mile where the stream went into a thick wooded area again. Beyond the woods he could see the terrain dip downward. "That valley is about five miles down land," he said. "We passed through it this morning."

"I remember." She nodded.

"You take the boy and go on. Your pa should be waiting there. If he isn't, you stay there and wait till I get there," Fargo told her.

"Where are you going?" she asked.

"I'm going to cut across and double back to where the Cheyenne attacked. It has to be on the way to the camp," Fargo said.

Her eyes studied him. "You don't think there'll be anybody waiting in the valley. You think they've all been killed, don't you?" she said.

He paused before replying. "It's possible," he said quietly, and she shook her head in disagreement.

"No, I know Bertram Thorgard. He's planned better than that," April said. "He'll survive."

"And I know the Cheyenne," Fargo said. "They won't be drawn into a trap. Besides, if he's waiting in the valley, I won't believe anything he tells me. I want to see what I can for myself, especially if Thunderhawk will come after us." He took a length of lariat out as he lifted the boy onto her saddle and tied the small wrists to the saddle horn. "Keep him tied or you'll be chasing him all over the woods and lose him," Fargo said.

She nodded and rode slowly away, sandy hair swaying to the rhythm of the horse.

He waited until she was out of sight before turning the Ovaro east. He rode hard, taking every shortcut he spotted, the way to the Cheyenne camp easy enough to find. He slowed as he drew near the sloping land that led to the forested plateau. Thorgard's plan had been to draw Thunderhawk out. He'd make his stand on the slope where his men could stay low and fire up at the Cheyenne, Fargo knew. He nudged the Ovaro over a low crest that led to another slope, and reined to a halt, his lips drawing back in disgust.

A handful of buzzards had begun to slowly wheel over the scene that lay before him. The slope was covered with the silent forms, the bodies of men in the grotesque, arrested positions of violent death. Thorgard's drifters lay scattered across the slope from side to side. But they were not alone. On the higher land beyond, the Cheyenne warriors lay, already placed in neat rows. The Cheyenne intended to return for their dead and build the traditional funeral pyre.

Fargo hastily guided the Ovaro forward, passing among the bodies of Thorgard's men. He counted as he rode and felt the distaste well up inside him, ending his count at thirty-four as he reached the middle of the slope. Thirty-four men, most with at least three arrows each in them. He spurred the horse on and came to a halt at the neat rows of Cheyenne warriors and counted again. Thunderhawk had lost twenty of his warriors, Fargo noted grimly, turning the Ovaro around to thread his way back through the carnage.

Thirty-four men lost . . . Fargo frowned in thought. Yet as bad a loss as it was, Thorgard had somehow managed to get away with half his force intact. The Ovaro moved sideways to avoid two men lying almost atop one another, and Fargo heard the sudden, pain-racked groan. He reined to a halt, leapt from the Ovaro, and saw the figure at his right twitch, the groan sound again. He took a long stride and sank down on one knee beside the man who somehow still lived, despite the two arrows that were embedded to the hilt in his chest. The man's eyes fluttered open, stared at him, and there was as much shock as pain in his gaze. "What happened to the others?" Fargo asked. "Did they get away?"

The man's lips moved and a little trickle of blood formed at the edge of his mouth. "Never," he breathed. "Never," and the word came on a hoarse, rasping whisper.

"Never what?" Fargo asked.

The man's lips moved, but the words took a long time to emerge. "Never came," he muttered. "Never came."

Fargo frowned. "What are you saying?" he pressed.

The man summoned a last burst of strength from his pierced body. "Thorgard," he whispered. "Told us to dig in . . . stay . . . while he came from the side with the others."

"But he never came up," Fargo finished, and the man's eyelids opened, fluttered closed, and his last breath was a shuddering, rasping sound.

Fargo rose, stepped to his horse, and swung into the saddle. He threaded his way back through the silent forms, turned down the slope, and when he reached the bottom, he sent the horse southwest. His jaw was a chiseled line as he thought about Bertram Thorgard and April's words: "He's planned . . . he'll survive," she had said. Thorgard had indeed planned. There was nothing unusual about a rearguard action, in and of itself. But this hadn't been a rearguard action. This had been deliberate deceit and trickery. Bertram Thorgard had sacrificed thirty-four men to buy himself time and distance.

Arrow fodder, Fargo remembered calling the men when he'd first seen them. Thorgard had grown angry, but the anger was because of his accuracy. Again, April's words came to mind: "Nothing is as it seems with him," she had said. Thirty-four men had found that out the hard way. Bertram Thorgard, Fargo decided, had to be given the kind of respect one gives a particularly powerful, particularly vicious and particularly cunning grizzly.

Fargo put the pinto into a gallop as he reached the low flat passages between the foothills. He cut through a pass between two peaks. The day was finding its end when he reached the valley and saw the stream glint in the last, slanting rays of the sun. He saw the horses, too, off to one side of the stream, their riders stretched out on the grass nearby with a row of six men standing guard in a loose circle. As he rode up, shapes took on definition.

April quickly got to her feet and watched him approach. The boy stood beside her, and as he reined to a halt, she came forward, her eyes searching his face. "I was so afraid you wouldn't come back, that something had happened to you," she said.

"Good sign, that," he said, and swung from the saddle to see Thorgard striding toward him, the man's heavy face an angry mask.

"Goddammit, Fargo, you'd no right to let her and the boy go on alone," Thorgard thundered.

"I knew she'd be safe and she had orders to wait for me if you didn't show," Fargo said.

"What the hell did you have to go back there for, anyway?" Thorgard questioned.

"Wanted to check out a few things for myself,"

Fargo answered. "Such as how many men Thunderhawk lost."

"You find that out?" Thorgard asked.

"Twenty," Fargo said.

"I could've made a guess at that," Thorgard muttered.

"Were you there?" Fargo slid at the man.

"Of course I was there," Thorgard snapped. "We fell back. That was the plan. The others just didn't make it." Fargo nodded and kept his silence. The man had no way of knowing he'd managed to learn the truth. He'd let it stay that way for now, Fargo told himself, and he saw Thorgard glance at the edge of the sun as it began to disappear behind the mountains. "Find us a cave big enough to hold three horses," he said. "There's got to be someplace in this valley that'll do."

"Only three horses?" Fargo asked mildly.

"That's right," Thorgard said. "I'll explain more later." He turned away and strode back to the men, and Fargo climbed onto the pinto as April watched.

"He's up to something again," she said.

"I can make a guess," Fargo said. "But let's wait and see. You stay with the boy."

"I already have my orders for that," she said, and Fargo sent the horse into a canter. The task wouldn't be that hard, he knew. The small valley was bordered with stone sides behind thick tree and brush cover. Caves were a natural part of that kind of terrain.

He rode to the right side of the valley and bent low in the saddle as he explored the thick foliage. He found three caves quickly but all were small, and he backtracked, rode northward, and in the fading light spotted the heavy growth of brush up on the rocky side of the land. He veered toward it, slowed, and saw the dark entranceway to the cave. It was all but hidden from sight by a dense growth of birch covering most of the cave, and he was able to ride into the opening without ducking his head.

He paused inside the cave and grunted in satisfaction. It was more than large enough and the dank scent of mold and dampness assailed his nostrils, along with the odor of weasel and raccoon urine. But it would do, and he turned and rode from the cave as dusk quickly deepened.

It was all but dark when he returned to the stream and saw Thorgard beside April, the boy a few paces away. The boy's wrists had been untied and he held a piece of beef jerky in one hand but his black eyes flung anger at Fargo.

"You find a cave?" Thorgard asked anxiously, and Fargo nodded. "You can take us later," Thorgard said.

"Who's us?" Fargo questioned.

"You, me, April, the boy, and three horses," the man answered.

"Aren't you staying to lead your men when Thunderhawk arrives, come morning? You know he'll come," Fargo said mildly.

"Yes, I expect he will," Thorgard said. "I've decided there's nothing to be gained by risking more lives fighting him. I've paid all the men off and told them that, come dawn, they're free to hightail it out of here."

"Bet that made them happy," Fargo remarked.

"It sure did. They'll be leaving with full pockets and pleased as larks, come dawn," Thorgard said.

"Only not for long," Fargo said, and drew an instant glare from Thorgard.

"What's that supposed to mean?" the man snapped. "I'm paying them off ahead of time and letting them ride away. What the hell's wrong about that?"

"I'll tell you what you're doing. You're going to have us hiding in that cave I found for you, safe and out of sight, when Thunderhawk arrives with his men. He'll naturally go after the men, figuring the boy's with them," Fargo said. "And he'll catch up to them. Even if they don't fight, if they just try to run, they won't have a chance. He'll kill every last one of them. Meanwhile, we'll be on our way with the boy. Same hand you played up in the mountains. Almost the same cards."

"I don't know that'll happen. Neither do you," the man said. "He might not catch up to them, and if he does, they might just outrun him. Or he might get tired of chasing after them."

"And the chicken might kill the hawk," Fargo grunted.

"I'll get my things and you can take us to that cave," Thorgard said, and strode away.

Fargo turned to find April's eyes on him.

"Is that what he did up in the mountains?" April asked, and he nodded. "And now we're all being part of more of the same," she said. "Isn't there anything you can do?"

"No," Fargo snapped, and heard the anger in his voice. "Not unless you want to get killed, too. Those drifters out there are doomed men and I can't help them. If they stay here to fight, they'll only be killed sooner. This way, a few might get away. Maybe. Thunderhawk will come and I can't stop that."

Frustration and despair showed in her face. "What

if you told them to hide nearby, too, find caves for themselves?"

Fargo's smile was grimly ironic. "Without tracks riding away from here, Thunderhawk will search every square inch of this area. He'll ferret them all out, and us too. Our only chance of staying alive is for them to ride out of here, just as Bertram Thorgard planned."

"And counted on you realizing the rotten, stinking truth of it," April said. "They're doomed, we're trapped in going along with him, and he wins again. Goddammit, I hate that man. He doesn't deserve to win, not ever."

Fargo made no reply as Thorgard came up leading his horse. He swung the boy onto the saddle and climbed up behind him. "He hasn't said a damn word yet," Thorgard muttered.

"I don't think he will, not for a long while," Fargo said as he started to lead the way across the narrow valley. The moon rose quickly and helped him find the cave again, and when the others were inside, he stepped out and broke off a young branch that bore a thick cluster of leaves. He used it to sweep away the hoofprints still on the ground, walked back a hundred yards or so, and finally returned to the cave. "Playing it safe," he said as he sat down. "If you're going to hide, hide well."

He glanced over at the boy and saw that his wrists had been tied again with a length of rawhide that stretched to April. "I'm going to get some sleep," Fargo said, and stretched out on the cool stone flooring of the cave.

"Yes, I want to get started as soon as possible, come morning," Thorgard said.

"Started for where?" Fargo frowned.

"I want to be in Colorado by day's end tomorrow, where the Yampa meets the Little Snake," Thorgard said. "I'll expect you to get us there."

"What's there?" Fargo asked.

"Safety," Thorgard said.

Fargo took in the reply; it told him little and he felt a stab of uneasiness. Thorgard was running far and hard to find safety. But then he was cunningly careful, Fargo reminded himself. Maybe April could help dispel the uneasiness that refused to be pushed aside. He closed his eyes and drew sleep around him and the cave became a silent place.

Dawn hadn't made its appearance yet when he woke, sat up, and pulled himself to his feet. Thorgard heard him and snapped awake at once, saw Fargo starting for the entrance of the cave. "Where are you going?" he hissed.

"Outside to watch," Fargo said.

"You crazy? You want to be seen?" Thorgard said.

"I don't plan to be seen," Fargo said. "But I plan to be sure Thunderhawk doesn't leave anyone back here on watch. I figure he's as canny as you are and then some."

"All right, but for Christ's sake be careful," the man snapped.

"I'm glad you care. I'm touched," Fargo said.

"I care about getting to Colorado," Thorgard said.

Fargo stepped from the cave, saw the first streaks of the dawn tinting the sky. He went into his long, loping stride and came to a halt beside a wide-branched hackberry that looked out across the narrow valley. He pulled himself high into the tree as the new day began to spread itself across the land. In the distance, he saw Thorgard's men waking, starting to mount up quickly, all eager to get away. He settled himself in the crotch of a branch and watched the men ride away. They headed east, spread out, setting an unhurried, casual pace. A deep sigh escaped him and he felt a grim anger inside himself. "Good luck, you poor bastards," he muttered aloud.

The Trailsman settled back in the tree as the sun rose. It edged over the horizon slowly, as if it were unwilling to witness to the slaughter that was almost certain to come. Fargo's eyes scanned the distant trees at the entrance to the valley and suddenly he sat up on the branch. Leaves moved in the distance, not in one place but in three places, and he saw the near-naked bronzed riders slowly emerge, each a hundred feet from the other. They moved out more boldly and one waved an arm. Fargo watched the cascade of Cheyenne pour out of the trees, Thunderhawk's handsome, powerful face sweeping the scene at once. He had almost all of his warriors with him, Fargo saw as he made a quick count and came up with some forty braves. He had replaced the twenty he'd lost in the initial attack, Fargo realized, and as he watched, the Cheyenne chief made a wide circle of the place where they had camped. He sent outriders out to scan the ground in all directions, and Fargo congratulated himself on having covered their tracks during the night.

Finally, Thunderhawk pointed east after the hoofprints that led down the valley. The small horde of Indian ponies swept after him as he raced on, and Fargo waited until they were out of sight. The Cheyenne had left no one behind.

Fargo climbed from the tree, then trotted back to the cave where everyone was awake and waiting. "Let's ride," he said, and watched as April took the boy onto the gray with her.

Thorgard brought up the rear as Fargo led the way from the cave and turned south at once. "We'll stay on this side of the divide," he said, and saw Thorgard nod.

Fargo set a steady pace and they soon left the cool forest places to ride in relatively open country. He halted to rest the horses frequently as the sun baked down with relentless glee. April rolled the bottom of her shirt up and he saw a flat, smooth waist, ribs showing just a little. She came up to ride beside him as the day grew longer and the boy in front of her sat in stoic silence.

"What's in Colorado?" Fargo asked her.

"I don't know," she said. "But he has a reason, you can be sure of that."

"Got any ideas?" he pressed.

"No, except to get away from Thunderhawk," April said.

"There's a good chance he's done that," Fargo said. "Thunderhawk may be satisfied with wiping out another thirty men."

"Good God, I hope so," April said, and he saw the tightness come into her face.

"There were things you didn't plan to talk about, you said. Changed your mind any now?" he asked.

Her hazel-flecked eyes glanced at him quickly and he saw the glint of unhappiness in their green depths. "No," she said quietly, and turned away. He nodded and rode on in silence. But she was still holding things back, he was certain. There were things still left unsaid, and he felt the uneasiness flood over him again.

He threw a glance back at Thorgard. The man rode with a kind of arrogant smugness on his heavy face, and Fargo felt himself agreeing more and more with April. Bertram Thorgard didn't deserve to win all the time. But then those who had absolutely no concern for anyone or anything always had a special corner on winning. Bastard, Fargo murmured silently as he spurred the pinto on toward Colorado Territory. And the uneasiness continued to ride with him.

6

It had been the kind of riding that takes the insides out of horse and rider—hard, hot, and heavy. The sun had begun to nod toward the horizon when they reached the irregularly shaped junction of the Yampa and Little Snake rivers. The land near the rivers lay flat, but to the left, thickly forested hills rose up in a jagged line. Fargo frowned in surprise as he saw the neat row of brown Morgans lined up along the bank of the Yampa, each groomed and saddled in the best U.S. Cavalry fashion. A troop of blue-uniformed figures camped near their mounts and a platoon pennant fluttered from a pole in the ground beside a small field tent. The pennant read: TROOP E—7TH U.S. CAVALRY.

Fargo saw April's face mirror his own surprise as Bertram Thorgard smiled and spurred his horse forward. "Leave it to the army to be on time," he murmured.

"You got a United States Cavalry platoon to meet you?" Fargo frowned incredulously.

"It pays to have friends in Washington," Thorgard said.

"All this just in case Thunderhawk shows up?" Fargo asked.

"I believe in being prepared. I'd have thought you'd have learned that by now," Thorgard snapped. He rode on, and Fargo's gaze went to the figure that stepped from the field tent. The figure wore lieutenant's bars on his blue uniform; he had neatly trimmed blond hair and looked as though he had only begun to shave.

"Mr. Thorgard?" the officer said as Thorgard dismounted in front of the tent. "I'm Lieutenant Tibbet."

"Glad to see you. I hope you haven't been waiting around too long," Thorgard said.

"Got here yesterday," the lieutenant said, and glanced at Fargo as the big man pulled the Ovaro to a halt, April and the boy beside him.

"This is Skye Fargo, the Trailsman," Thorgard introduced them. "And April Thorgard." He gestured to the boy as April set him on the ground. "And the boy's the reason you're here, Lieutenant," he said.

"Step into the tent and tell me about it," Lt. Tibbet said. "Whatever the problem is, I'm sure we can handle it." The lieutenant didn't even try to avoid sounding officious.

"Protecting the boy is the problem," Thorgard said. "We took him from a Cheyenne chief named Thunderhawk. The chief is determined to take him back."

"He'll be pretty far from Cheyenne country to follow you all the way down here," the lieutenant said.

"Yes, but I can't take any chances. I must assume he'll try again, if only to save face," Thorgard said.

"How many braves does he have with him?" Lt. Tibbet asked, and Thorgard looked to Fargo.

"About forty," Fargo said.

The lieutenant's smooth, young face took on a faintly chiding air. "I have fifty troopers, disciplined and well-armed. With our firepower I don't anticipate any problem with this wandering Indian."

"You ever fight the Cheyenne, Lieutenant?" Fargo asked mildly.

"No, not actually," Tibbet answered. "But I don't believe any undisciplined horde can stand up to proper military tactics."

"That's the trouble with the Cheyenne. Their tactics are not at all proper," Fargo said.

The lieutenant's tone was one of patient tolerance. "You can be assured of the boy's safety now," he said.

"That makes me feel real good," Fargo said, backing from the tent and leading the Ovaro away.

"Wait," he heard April call after him, and he saw her follow, dragging the boy along with her. He waited for her to catch up and then walked on. "You think Lieutenant Tibbet is an ass, don't you?" she said.

"Bull's-eye," he grunted.

Her eyes swept the troopers not far away as Fargo halted. "You can't compare them to those drifters. They're better trained and better armed. That has to make a difference," April said.

"Yes. They'll die more disciplined," Fargo muttered harshly.

April frowned at him. "Is that all? Isn't there a bright side?"

"Maybe," he conceded. "Thunderhawk won't know they're led by an inexperienced officer. But he will know that any direct engagement with a strong cavalry troop is sure to lose him a lot of warriors. He may take one look, decide it's not worth all the trouble, and leave." Fargo looked across at the field tent where Thorgard and the lieutenant still conversed. "Fact is, I don't think he'll show. Daddy went overboard this time," he said.

April stared into space. "He plans too carefully for that," she murmured.

Fargo shrugged, looked at the boy, and spoke to him in Siouan. He received only a stony silence in return.

"What did you ask him?" April questioned.

"I asked him his name. You heard his answer," Fargo commented.

She nodded, looking back toward the field tent. Lt. Tibbet and Thorgard had stepped outside as dusk slid across the land. Thorgard squinted through the half-light, saw April with Fargo, and beckoned to her. "I have to get back. I'm sure he and the lieutenant have some plans for keeping the boy tonight and they'll include me," April said.

Fargo pointed to a hillock where a long box elder spread its wide branches. "I'll be bedding down over there," he said. " 'Case you want to come visiting."

She frowned at him, protest in her eyes. "That's not fair. You know he'll have me stay with the boy," she said.

"Maybe you'll get a night off," Fargo said, and she made a wry sound. "Would you come visiting if you could?" he asked slyly.

The hazel-flecked eyes studied him for a moment. "I think I'll just let you wonder about that," she said, turned, and sauntered away, the boy in front of her.

He watched the willowy figure sway, the flat, tight bottom both prim and provocative. "Maybe I'll come up with the wrong answer," he called.

"How will you know?" she tossed back without turning, and he watched her cross to where the lieutenant had two troopers setting up a pup tent. The boy walked at her side, still very hostile and uncooperative but more willing to be with April than anyone else. Thorgard had been right about that, too, Fargo reflected as he walked on to the distant hillock.

Darkness rolled over the land and Fargo settled down under the low, wide branches of the box elder. At the camp, a cooking fire glowed, a small circle of soft orange in the darkness. The troopers lined up for dinner were so many wavering shapes and shadows. Fargo set out his bedroll, munched on cold beef jerky, and watched the distant fire begin to burn down. April and the boy were no doubt in the pup tent, and Fargo saw the two sentries the lieutenant had set out, one at each end of the camp.

He let a grim sound escape his lips. The lieutenant was showing his lack of experience. But it didn't really matter, Fargo realized. He was convinced that Thunderhawk wouldn't follow them this distance. And if he did, he wouldn't arrive till morning. He'd have to go slow, watch the trail, make certain he didn't make a mistake. It'd take time, too much time and too much effort. Thunderhawk would break off the pursuit and return to his own camp. Sixty slain intruders would make for more than enough coup stories around the long winter campfires. And more than enough revenge.

Fargo undressed, slid into his bedroll, and closed his eyes. The night stayed still and peaceful and he slept well. When he woke, the morning sun glistened on the rivers where they came together, and a distant goldfinch sang in its clear, pure voice.

Fargo rose, went up along the bank of the Yampa, and found a spot to bathe. He let the sun quickly bake him dry. When he returned to the campsite, morning coffee was on and some of the troopers were already polishing their gear. He took a tin mug of coffee a sergeant offered, and he had just drained the bracing brew when April came from the pup tent with the boy in tow. The boy chewed on a piece of johnnycake and April paused to exchange pleasantries with Lt. Tibbet. She continued past her father, and Fargo waited as she sauntered toward him. In a deep-blue shirt that hugged the long breasts, she looked fresh as a tall larkspur.

Her green eyes danced as she halted before him. "Did you spend a sleepless night wondering?" she asked.

"You spend it regretting?" Fargo countered, and she laughed.

"You won't know that, either," she answered, and suddenly he saw the laughter fade from her eyes. She stared past him and he saw her lips drop open. He turned, following her gaze to the hills. The lone horseman stood silent and still, outlined against the new sun, the black-coal eyes burning down from the handsome face. Fargo felt astonishment flood through him as he stared up at the bronzed figure on the brown horse.

"I'll be dammed," he murmured. But others had suddenly become aware of the figure on the hill, and he heard Lt. Tibbet's voice cut through the flurry of activity.

"Mount up," the lieutenant called out, and the troopers swung onto their horses.

Fargo saw Thorgard appear, stare up at the lone

figure, and the man's heavy face almost wore a look of anticipation. As Fargo continued to stare up into the hills, the lone figure was suddenly not alone as a line of Cheyenne braves moved into sight on both sides of Thunderhawk. They halted and looked down at the campsite, and Fargo made a quick count that once again totaled forty braves.

Lt. Tibbet passed in front of him on his mount, rode to the head of his troopers, and started to raise one arm into the air when the Cheyenne turned almost as one and vanished from the ridge. The lieutenant lowered his arm slowly and stared up at the hills. "Double formation. Prepare for an attack," the lieutenant ordered.

"Relax," Fargo said. "He's not going to attack now."

The lieutenant frowned at him. "What makes you so sure of that?" he questioned.

"I know the Cheyenne way," Fargo said. "He just lets you know he's there. He'll keep doing that for a spell and hope it makes you nervous."

"Well, that won't happen. I'll go up there after him and put an end to this foolishness right now," the lieutenant said.

"He'd like that, too," Fargo remarked mildly.

The lieutenant shot him an annoyed glance and turned to Thorgard. "My orders are that I'm at your complete disposal for four days, Mr. Thorgard. Do you want me to take care of this Indian right now?" he asked.

"No, let's hold off on that, Lieutenant," Thorgard said, keeping his face expressionless. "I realized I could only have your services for a limited time. That's why I arranged to have you meet me here. I want your protection until I reach Dead Horse Point in Utah Territory. Fargo will take us along the best trail."

"No problem there, Mr. Thorgard," Lt. Tibbet said. "You'll reach it and be safe all the way. Let's get started." He turned, barked orders to his troopers in a firm, confident voice. "Form a double column, four troopers riding rear guard," he said. "Mr. Thorgard, Miss April, and the boy will ride in between the two columns at all times."

Fargo mounted the pinto, Thorgard and April swung in between the two rows of troopers, and the lieutenant waved the column forward. Skye saw the boy turn and look across at the hills, and in the small, stern face he saw the shadow of a smile.

His own jaw set, Fargo spurred the Ovaro on past the front of the double column and headed southwest. He rode ahead, dropped back, mostly kept in sight of the troopers as he waved them forward to the best trails opening up before him.

The land grew flat and dry as they neared Utah Territory. He saw the thin column of dust to the west and shook his head in consternation. Thunderhawk and his warriors were keeping pace. As the lieutenant called a halt to refresh the horses at a stream, the column of dust dwindled away. The Cheyenne had halted also.

Fargo rode back to where April sat beside the boy, four troopers forming a ring around them. "He's staying with us," Fargo said to her. "Why, goddammit?" he swore suddenly.

"You said he'd think a long time before making a direct attack on a full cavalry troop," April reminded him. "Maybe he's still trying to make up his mind."

"Maybe," Fargo said, unable to dismiss the answer entirely. "But he's taking a hell of a long time about it." His eyes swept the land in the direction of the

Cheyenne. "It doesn't make any damn sense for him to even be here." Fargo frowned. "The boy was a prize captive, treated special, but he couldn't be that much of a prize. Thunderhawk's had enough revenge for ten prize captives. Why is he here, dammit?"

April shrugged, turned away quickly, and the lieutenant's voice interrupted. "Mount up," he called, and April almost leapt to her feet and took the saddle with the boy. Fargo watched her with narrowed eyes. She'd been glad for the interruption, afraid of more questioning. What the hell was she holding back? he wondered and felt the anger stab at him. Whatever it was, he'd have to find a way to press her harder—and damn soon, he grunted.

He turned the Ovaro south and started to ride on when he halted, noticing that the thin column of dust had suddenly spiraled and changed direction. It headed toward the troopers and within moments he saw the Cheyenne racing across the ground. Lt. Tibbet saw them also, and Fargo heard his voice bark commands as he wheeled his mount around. "Prepare to attack," he snapped, and Fargo saw the troopers bring their horses around with smart precision. His gaze went back to the Cheyenne and he unholstered the Colt with a frown as the Indians continued to race toward the column. As they drew near, they took on individual form. Thunderhawk was not among them, he saw, and he guessed there were not more than twenty braves in the attacking force. The air reverberated as the troopers laid down a volley of fire. Too soon, Fargo murmured—the Cheyenne were still out of range.

As he watched, flicking a glance to April and the boy, who were huddled behind the troopers, the Cheyenne wheeled, rode parallel to the troopers, and continued to stay just out of range. They kept racing on, then suddenly turned and galloped away.

Lt. Tibbet spurred his mount forward, started to motion for pursuit, and reined up as he saw the second band of Cheyenne racing toward him from the other side of the column. "Rearguard troops face left," he called, and almost half the platoon whirled around to face the new attacks. Again, Fargo searched the oncoming Cheyenne and saw that Thunderhawk was not among them. In almost an exact repetition of the first attack, the second band drew close and wheeled away without answering the volley of gunfire.

They disappeared across the flatland and Fargo dropped the Colt back into its holster.

Lt. Tibbet drew a long breath. The officer fixed his gaze on Fargo and spurred his mount closer. "You say you know the Cheyenne? What was that all about?" he asked.

"It was about testing, to see what it'd take to draw you out," Fargo answered. "And each time they make another pass you'll have to wonder whether it's just more testing or for real until you're ready to jump out of your skin."

"We'll see about that," Lt. Tibbet snapped, and wheeled his horse away. "Columns forward as before," he called out, and the troopers reformed quickly, with Thorgard, April, and the boy inside the double columns.

Fargo rode on ahead, never too far to be within sight of the troop, and he was beside them when the Cheyenne suddenly made another swoop. They raced in as before, drew even closer than the first time, circled the platoon, and finally raced away as the rifle fire fell short.

"Cease fire," the lieutenant called out, holding his mount in tight control. Fargo saw the thin line of perspiration that coated his forehead.

Tibbet ordered the platoon forward again, and Fargo galloped on ahead, finding a shallow dip in the land where a thick stand of hackberry and elm lined both sides. The day was drawing to a close, and the lieutenant was glad to call a rest in the coolness of the shallow valley. "We'll make camp here for the night," he said. "It'll be dark before the hour's up."

Fargo dismounted and took his horse to one side.

The lieutenant ordered his troopers to sleep in a square and placed the pup tent for April and the boy in the center of the square. "Sentries every fifty yards, four-hour shifts," he ordered.

"I'll bed down right here beside the tent," Thorgard said.

"I'll take the other side," the lieutenant added, and turned to April. "I assure you, you'll be perfectly safe," he told her with sweeping confidence.

Fargo grunted inwardly. The lieutenant was right, but not for the reasons he thought. The Cheyenne didn't mount all-out night attacks. They did other things. Fargo grimaced and sat down as a small cooking fire was lighted.

April stayed close to the boy, he saw, her face set and unsmiling, and she made no move to come over to him. In truth, she studiously avoided meeting his gaze. He waited, relaxed, and when darkness came, he shared in the army rations of soup and hardtack. As he finished, he saw Thorgard step over to April and the boy.

"I'm tying him hand and foot tonight," Thorgard said. "I'm not having him try to run out there."

April glanced over at Fargo as he strolled toward her. "You think that's necessary?" she asked, and he nodded. April turned away, her lips tight as she shot a sullen glance at her father.

"The boy's warmed up to me a little. That's why you brought me along, to handle him. Tying him up like a pig will ruin whatever I've managed to accomplish," she said.

"Tie him," Thorgard snapped, and handed her two lengths of rawhide thongs. She rose and started into the tent with the boy.

"I'll do it," Fargo said. "That way he won't blame you directly." She shrugged and he followed her into the tent, kneeling down as he began to tie the boy's wrists.

April watched, finally lowering herself to the ground beside him.

"Why is Thunderhawk so damn determined to take the boy back?" Fargo asked her.

"We went through that already," April said.

"He's not looking any longer, not making up his mind. He'll attack. He's just trying to make the lieutenant fight his way," Fargo said. "Why, goddammit? Why is he willing to take on a full cavalry platoon?"

"I guess he's just very vengeful," April said, not looking at him.

"Try again, honey," Fargo bit out.

Bertram Thorgard interrupted as he pushed his head into the tent. "You finished, dammit? Let's get some shut-eye," he said.

"In a second," Fargo answered, testing the tightness of the thongs. He rose to his feet, reached down, and pulled April up without gentleness. "We'll talk tomorrow night. I'll find a way. You're holding something back, and you better figure to tell me or I'm pulling out. My job's finished, anyway."

April's eyes grew wide at once. "No, don't," she said. "You can't."

"Why the hell not?" he hissed.

"Because I'm afraid," she said. "And somehow, I'm less afraid when you're around."

"Then you loosen your little tongue tomorrow night," Fargo said, and started to turn away. He halted and yanked her against him. He pressed his lips hard against her mouth and felt surprise give way to softness as the long breasts were soft against his chest. "That's to help loosen it," he said as he stepped back and strode from the tent.

Thorgard, waiting outside, fastened narrowed eyes on him. "You and April are getting real chummy, it seems," the man said.

"Those who raid together trade together," Fargo said cheerfully, and saw Thorgard's eyes take on a baleful stare.

"You just see that we get to Dead Horse Point in four days," he growled.

"That may not be exactly up to me," Fargo commented.

"You just do your job. I'll see that Tibbet doesn't do anything stupid. When the time's right, I'll let him finish that goddamn Indian," Thorgard said.

"Just like that," Fargo grunted.

"He's got the firepower to do it," Thorgard said.

"He has that," Fargo agreed as he walked away. He took the Ovaro off to the far corner of the square of troopers as the men bedded down for the night. He put a blanket on the ground, took off shirt and boots, and put his gun belt next to him. He lay awake for a while as the camp grew still and finally let himself sleep.

He woke with the first change of sentries and again with the second. When he returned to sleep, his hand rested on the Colt at his side, and it stayed there until the morning sun came to wake him with its new warmth.

He rose, heard the camp stir into wakefulness, started to gather his things to go to the river when he heard the shout. It was one of the troopers from the far corner of the camp.

"My God, oh, Jesus," he heard the young voice groan. "Lieutenant. Oh, God, over here."

Fargo saw Tibbet appear from the back side of the tent, still buttoning his uniform trousers as he rushed to where a half-dozen of his men had already gathered. Fargo walked after him slowly, felt the deep sigh rush from him.

"Goddamn," he heard Tibbet say.

April came out from the tent. Fargo walked on, Thorgard hurrying after him, and the lieutenant turned, his young face drained of color. "Two of the sentries and three troopers," the lieutenant said. "Their throats cut. Two with arrows in them." He kept his eyes on Fargo almost accusingly. "Nobody heard anything. They killed the three men while they were asleep."

"After they killed the sentries," Fargo said.

"Those stinking savages," the lieutenant said, and his voice shook with a mixture of anger and distaste. "They come charging at us today and I'll put an end to their games once and for all. I'll ride every one of them into the ground," he vowed.

"Just what he wants you to do," Fargo said calmly.

"Get mad and do something real stupid." The lieutenant frowned back. "You'll have to leave at least a dozen men behind to protect the boy," Fargo said. "That means you'll divide your forces and weaken both. He can pick and choose which one he'll hit."

"Murdering my men at night will weaken my forces, too," the lieutenant returned.

"We can pretty much stop that," Fargo said.

"How?"

"We'll talk about that when night comes, if you don't play into his hands before," Fargo said, and turned away. He walked back to April and she stared at him, her eyes wide with horror.

"Five young men just murdered," she breathed. "God, how horrible."

"A cougar fights in its own ways, a hawk in its ways," Fargo said. "Tonight," he added, and moved on.

He took the Ovaro, went upstream, and bathed. When he returned, the lieutenant was ready to pull out. Skye saw the five graves placed at one side of the valley and the men lined up silently in two columns.

Fargo rode on ahead, found a direct route to the level Tayaputs Plateau, and had the column making good time when he saw the line of bronzed horsemen appear from the north. They gathered speed, forming into two bands, but both stayed on the same side of the columns this time. Fargo slowed and returned to the columns as Lt. Tibbet watched the Cheyenne draw closer. Skye moved his horse over to where Tibbet could see him, scanned the onrushing bronzed horsemen. This time he saw Thunderhawk in the lead, the Cheyenne's handsome, chiseled face stark and severe, his black eyes boring through the columns of men.

"Prepare to fire," Tibbet barked. "Columns left."

The platoon wheeled, took up positions, and Tibbet fired a shot from his army Smith & Wesson. His men followed with a thunderous volley, and the Cheyenne peeled away, circled, and started a direct, head-on charge. Fargo saw the Indians flatten themselves on their ponies and heard the lieutenant shouting commands. "This is it, they're coming in. Fire at will," he shouted.

Fargo watched as the Cheyenne raced toward the platoon and suddenly swerved, raced away to the left as the fusillade of rifle fire fell short. They made a wide circle and continued to run until they disappeared over a low hill.

Tibbet stared after Thunderhawk, his face soaked with perspiration. He slowly relaxed, sank back in the saddle, and wiped his brow with the sleeve of his uniform. There was anger and a touch of fear in the glance he shot at Fargo before he quickly pulled his eyes away. "Column resume march," he called out.

Fargo turned the Ovaro forward as the platoon regrouped into two columns again. He rode on, found a dry trail across broken ground, and guessed they'd ridden for perhaps another two hours when he saw the bronzed figures suddenly appear over the top of the small dune.

The Cheyenne gathered speed quickly and were in a full-out charge in seconds and he saw Thunderhawk's strong-planed face in the lead.

Lt. Tibbet reacted instantly, shouting commands as the platoon fell into battle formation. The charging Cheyenne raced past with a thunder of hooves and sudden war cries, continued on, and vanished from sight over a low hill.

"Goddamn murdering cowards," the lieutenant screamed after them. "Come on and fight." He spurred his mount forward, saw Fargo nearby, and reined to a halt, his face flushed, his lips quivering. He gathered his horse in, turned, and regained control of himself with a deep breath. "Column forward as before," he called out.

Fargo glanced at Thorgard and saw that the man's heavy face was drawn in, his eyes narrowed in thought.

The day moved toward an end and Fargo found a place where the Green River curved east inside Utah Territory. There was enough flat, open land at one side along the river and a thick stand of firs a hundred yards back.

The Lieutenant brought his troops to a halt and set up camp. Fargo saw the drained stare stay in his eyes. Two troopers put up the pup tent and Fargo watched Thorgard and April face each other off to one side. He could only hear muttered words in angry tones, April spitting out sentences with icy fury and Thorgard waving his arms threateningly as he raged at her. As Fargo watched, he saw April's anger begin to crumble, her resolve falter under Thorgard's onslaught, and she grew silent, submission sliding across her face. When she turned away and strode to the tent with the boy, her shoulders sagged in defeat.

She disappeared into the tent as dusk deepened into night and Lt. Tibbet came toward Fargo. "You said you knew how to stop those sneaking savages from murdering my men while they sleep," Tibbet said.

"You need light so your sentries can see," Fargo said. "Circle the camp with enough kindling wood to make a ring of fire. Put your sentries back twenty-five feet inside the circle. Nobody will be able to get over or through the fire without stepping into the light. No getting through, no sneaking up on anyone."

"Ingenious," the lieutenant said.

"It works against wolves. It'll work against Cheyenne," Fargo said, and the lieutenant hurried away with a sense of relief in his face. Fargo heard him barking orders as he sat down beside the Ovaro. He relaxed for a long hour and then started from the camp as the ring of fire was lighted.

"Where are you going?" Tibbet frowned at him.

"Scout some on my own," Fargo answered, and jumped the low flames with the Ovaro to trot into the darkness. The answer had been honest enough, but he also wanted to allow some time for the camp to settle down to sleep before he paid April a visit. He moved the pinto to the bank of the river and rode slowly and carefully south, his eyes scanning the land under the pale silver light of a half-moon. Thunderhawk had made only unnerving probes up to now. If the lieutenant's nerve held out, the Cheyenne would have to do more. If Tibbet cracked, Thunderhawk would have things his way. In any case, the time for reckoning was drawing close, and Fargo surveyed the terrain they'd have to travel, come morning. He made mental notes as he rode, taking in hills, ridges, heavy forest cover along the edges of the river. Finally he turned back and slowly rode to where he saw the ring of fire in the darkness.

The Cheyenne would have seen it, of course, and realized the foolishness of trying to slip close to the campsite. They'd turn away and let the night continue.

As he neared the low flames, Fargo slowed further, brought the Ovaro to the edge of the ring, and saw one of the sentries raise his carbine. "Hold your fire," Fargo called out. He sent the horse over the flame and the sentry relaxed visibly.

Fargo rode into the sleeping camp, swung to the ground, and walked to the pup tent to find four troopers on guard around it. "She's expecting me," Fargo said.

"Sorry, no visitors," the soldier said. "Nobody goes in. Nobody."

"Who's order was that?" Fargo frowned.

"The lieutenant's, sir," the trooper said.

"Was it, now?" Fargo growled, and stepped past the trooper as he headed around to the other side of the tent. He spied Tibbet's sleeping form near the rear corner of the tent. Skye took a long stride when the voice cut into the stillness.

"No need to wake him up," it said, and Fargo turned to see Bertram Thorgard standing nearby. "He was just following my instructions," the man said.

"You afraid of something?" Fargo slid at Thorgard.

"Not a thing," the man snapped. "But April's a funny girl. Questions make her nervous, and when she gets nervous, she'll be more trouble than help."

"And you aim to see I don't bother her with any questions," Fargo said.

"That's right. Stay away from her, Fargo. You got questions, you ask me," Thorgard said.

"Something stinks here, besides you. I'm going to find out, I can promise you that," Fargo returned.

"Just leave her alone. She's here to take care of the boy. That's all she's going to do," Thorgard said.

"She's going to be ducking a lot of arrows doing it, and I want to know why," Fargo said.

"Because that goddamn Indian is a crazy man,"

Thorgard said. "He figures we made a laughingstock of him by taking the boy, and he has to get him back to save face. If you can't see that, you don't know Indians. Now don't bother me anymore, dammit."

Thorgard spun on his heel and strode away, and Fargo watched him go, making a bitter sound with his lips. The man's indignation was almost real, just as his explanations were almost reasonable. But Fargo heard April's warning as it leapt in his mind once again: "Nothing ever is as it seems with Bertram Thorgard." That applied to reasonable explanations also, he was certain, and he began to walk back to where he'd left the Ovaro. Thorgard had closed April away from him, but he had to know it would only last the night. He couldn't watch her every minute. Maybe he hoped the Cheyenne would turn away, finally, and make the answers unimportant. It was possible, Fargo admitted as he took his blanket down. But he wouldn't take bets on it.

He lay down, stretched out, shed his outer clothing, and let sleep come to him, certain of only two things: he'd find a way to reach April, and the day wouldn't bring peace and quiet.

7

He exchanged glances with April over morning coffee as the platoon prepared to ride. In her eyes he saw inner turmoil, pain, fear, apology, and bitter frustration. He passed close to her as she lifted the boy into the saddle, with Thorgard watching as a diamondback watches a field mouse. "I'll find a way," Fargo muttered without pausing, and knew she heard though she held her face expressionless.

He swung onto the pinto and rode on ahead of the platoon as the troopers formed the double column again. He'd only gone a few dozen feet when he saw the Cheyenne appear, form two columns, and begin to ride parallel to the platoon. He saw the tall, powerful figure of the Indian chief at the head of his braves, his black-coal eyes burning across the space between him and the platoon.

Fargo motioned for the lieutenant to follow him along the edge of the riverbank. As the platoon moved to the right to do so, the Cheyenne moved with them, keeping perhaps a hundred yards' distance between them.

Fargo rode point, and the platoon followed, Lt. Tibbet at its head; Tibbet kept glancing nervously across at the Cheyenne. Skye turned his eyes back to the trail he had roughly scanned during the night. There was no need to wonder where the Cheyenne might suddenly appear, he thought wryly. They were in full view, moving quietly along with the platoon. He fell back to where the lieutenant rode a few paces in front of the double column, and he saw the tension in the man's young face.

"Put the platoon into a slow trot," Fargo said, spurring the pinto forward as the troopers increased speed at the lieutenant's command. Fargo glanced across at the Cheyenne and watched as they put their ponies into a slow trot. He let the platoon come up behind him. "Go into a walk," he said, and Tibbet gave the command. Fargo's gaze stayed on Thunderhawk and saw the Cheyenne put his pony into a walk. He smiled as he glanced back at the lieutenant.

"What are they doing, goddammit?" Tibbet barked.

"Riding," Fargo said, and sent the Ovaro forward into a canter. The lieutenant did the same with his troopers and Fargo saw the Cheyenne keep pace at once. It was a deadly game, he realized, and it would end soon. He glanced back at the lieutenant and saw the younger man's eyes constantly flick to the Cheyenne who rode almost serenely in place. Tibbet's lips moved as he muttered silently and Fargo eyed the Cheyenne again. In some intuitive way, Thunderhawk knew that the lieutenant was close to the breaking point. He would keep the pressure on until the very last moment.

Fargo's glance went to the sun. They'd make Dead Horse Point by sundown if they could maintain a steady pace. But that was growing damned unlikely, he grimaced. There was a trading post and a blacksmith at Dead Horse Point, not much else, but Thorgard had a reason for wanting to reach there before he lost the protection of the cavalry troop. Thorgard always had a reason, he had learned—the man was as wily as he was unprincipled.

Fargo rode on ahead, surveying the terrain. He had halted to water the pinto when the troop pulled to a stop. "Tank up," he said. "We leave the river and go southeast from here."

Tibbet nodded, peering nervously across at the Cheyenne as he let the horses drink and the men refill their canteens. Thunderhawk had halted, sat quietly, patiently, and when the platoon moved forward again, he rode forward with his braves, still perfectly paralleling the double column. The lieutenant put his troopers into a trot as he glared over at the Cheyenne, and Fargo watched the sun begin to slide down toward the horizon. Maybe two, three hours of daylight left, he murmured to himself, enough to reach Dead Horse Point, but he suddenly felt his stomach begin to grow tight. Thunderhawk had played his hand out and the lieutenant had held fast. Nervous, on the thin edge of breaking, the lieutenant still held on. Thunderhawk would have to make his move soon, Fargo knew.

He spurred the pinto into a gallop and rode on, his eyes sweeping the terrain until he spied the series of stratified rock formations running horizontally across the ground. The bottom layer formed a long, deep cut with a ledge overhead tall enough for horse and rider.

He wheeled the Ovaro around and rode back to

meet the column. With a quick glance over at the Cheyenne, he reined up beside the lieutenant and spoke in quick, tight commands. "Time could be running out. There's a good place to make a stand. Get this troop moving," he said. To emphasize his words, he turned and sent the Ovaro into a gallop. He glanced back and saw Tibbet motion the columns to follow.

Fargo looked across and saw Thunderhawk put his ponies into a gallop. Maybe they'd get lucky, Fargo muttered prayerfully. Maybe the Cheyenne wouldn't see the deep cut until it was too late. But another quick glance across the open space separating him from the Cheyenne let him see Thunderhawk peering ahead, and as the stratified rock formations came into sight, he saw the Indian chief peer harder.

The deep cut came into sight, close enough to reach, he estimated, when he saw Thunderhawk wheel his brown mount, lift his arm high, and the sturdy Indian ponies wheeled after him. The wild, sharp war cries split the air. No more fake passes, Fargo saw. Thunderhawk charged to do battle this time, aware that perhaps his last opportunity would be gone if the platoon reached the deep cut.

Fargo threw a quick glance back at the lieutenant and saw Tibbet's eyes widen as he watched the onrushing Cheyenne.

"Don't stop. Run for it. We can make it," Fargo shouted back as he kept the Ovaro racing across the ground. But he saw Tibbet draw his rifle, wheeling his mount around to face the onrushing Cheyenne.

"Fire at will," Tibbet shouted. "Charge the bastards." He sent his mount racing forward, and his troopers wheeled and followed him, rifles raised, firing as they charged.

"No, goddammit," Fargo shouted but knew his voice was drowned out by the gunfire. He reined up as Thunderhawk let his braves peel off in two waves, one to the right, the other to the left, and raced away as the two lines converged.

"After them," the lieutenant shouted. "We'll finish them."

"Don't chase them, you damn fool," Fargo shouted into the gunfire and cursed under his breath.

Lt. Tibbet was leading his platoon in full pursuit as the Cheyenne raced over a low hill. Fargo saw Thorgard beside April and the boy, uncertainty in his heavy face. Fargo waved frantically at the man as he raced back toward him. April saw him first and sent the gray galloping forward. Thorgard followed, and as the gunfire exploded on the other side of the low hill, Fargo led the others to the long, deep cut. A half-wall of rock rose up before the cut and he vaulted the natural wall, reined up, and was on the ground, the big Sharps in his hand, as April came in with the boy and Thorgard followed.

"Goddamn, he should've left a dozen men with us," Thorgard protested as he slid from his horse.

"The lieutenant figures he'll take care of Thunderhawk," Fargo said.

"He ought to, dammit. He's got the guns and the men," Thorgard snapped.

"Along with the army field-tactics manual and a bad case of nerves. Neither of which will help him fight the Cheyenne," Fargo said. "Stay down behind those rocks," he ordered April, and she sank down with the boy beside her.

Fargo peered past her out to the hillside as two troopers crested the top, riding like the devil with four Cheyenne chasing them. Another two near-naked forms appeared from the right side to box in the fleeing soldiers.

"You stay here," Fargo said as he leapt onto the Ovaro and sent the horse vaulting from the hiding place. He raced the Ovaro at a full gallop and started to warn the fleeing troopers. Tightening his thighs against the Ovaro's ribs, he fired off two shots, and one of the Cheyenne flew sideways from his pony. Another fell forward over his pony's neck, bounced twice, and fell to the ground. The other two bronze-skinned horsemen fell away, and Fargo's third shot went in between them. He tried to draw a bead on one of them, but the Indian flattened himself onto his pony as it raced over the low hill. Fareo held his fire. The fourth Indian had disappeared farther down over the hill and Fargo saw the two troopers shift course and head toward him.

The sounds of gunfire were still heavy coming from the other side of the hill. Fargo spurred the Ovaro upward as the two troopers fell in behind him. He crested the rise, slowed, and saw the hillside strewn with blue uniforms and near-naked forms while, along the bottom of the slope, some two dozen troopers pursued a much smaller band of Cheyenne toward a stand of thick birch. Skye glimpsed the lieutenant at the head of the racing troopers, but he couldn't tell whether Thunderhawk was among the Cheyenne.

The two young troopers reined up beside him, their wide and fearful eyes looking to him for direction. "This way," he said, and wheeled the pinto back over the crest of the hill and down the other side.

"What about the lieutenant?" one asked, plainly out of a sense of duty.

"The lieutenant's trying to chase down Thunderhawk. He'll either do it or he won't. We won't make a difference either way," Fargo said, and sent the pinto racing downhill and back toward the deep cut.

Thorgard stood up when Fargo reached the overhang and jumped the low rock wall. The two troopers followed him in and jumped from their horses to crouch behind the rocks, their rifles in hand. Thorgard stared at them, lifted his eyes to Fargo.

"These the only two left?" He frowned.

"No, the lieutenant's still trying to run down Cheyenne," Fargo said. "But he hasn't a hell of a lot of men left."

"What about Thunderhawk?" Thorgard questioned.

Fargo shrugged. "Maybe yes, maybe no. I saw a lot of dead Cheyenne," he said. "But I saw more dead troopers."

"They broke off in little groups," one of the troopers said, shock and awe still in his voice. "The lieutenant had us attack in strength, but it was like swatting flies. They'd dart in, fire, bring down two or three men, and race away. They came in from all sides, hit and run, and come in again."

"But we got a lot of them," the other trooper said, no pride in his voice, only a terrible weariness. "They had to come in close. We couldn't help but get a lot of them."

"What now?" Thorgard broke in.

"We wait here," Fargo said.

"What for?" Thorgard pressed.

"To see who else will be going on with us," Fargo said.

"The hell with that. I want to get to Dead Horse Point," Thorgard said.

"It's over finally," April said. "You've won again." The bitterness came into her voice instantly.

"I don't take chances. You know that. Let's get moving," Thorgard said.

"Soon enough," Fargo growled.

Thorgard glared at him but fell silent, and Fargo's eyes turned to the distant hillside. The land was still now, with a tomblike stillness where not even a catbird sang. The sun had dipped to the horizon when Fargo saw the horsemen come into sight over the top of the hill and he counted seven blue uniforms. They rode slowly, and as they neared, he saw Lt. Tibbet's young face in the lead. Only the youth was gone from it, in his eyes a staring numbness that would never completely go away, Fargo knew. The seven riders came closer, and Fargo rose to his feet, climbed onto the pinto, and rode from under the rock ledge. The two troopers followed him and he glanced back to see Thorgard slowly come out with April and the boy.

He reined up in front of Lt. Tibbet and saw a trickle of blood from the tear in his uniform just below his left shoulder. Some of the others also had superficial wounds.

Tibbet stared at him as he spoke, each word more an effort of the spirit than the body. "We had them in the woods," he said. "I heard them right in front of us, running away. I could see their horses and we were catching them, and suddenly they were on foot, pouring arrows into us from both sides."

Fargo grunted grimly. "Two riders stayed with the horses, kept them running. The rest jumped off and ambushed you as you went past chasing their horses," he said.

"I got one," Tibbet said, and gestured to the trooper

beside him. "Fletcher got two. Then we had to run. They were all over and we couldn't even see them to shoot at."

"Thunderhawk, did you get him?" Fargo asked.

"I don't know," Tibbet said. "I don't know. I think so, but I'm not sure."

"Let's get out of here," Bertram Thorgard broke in.

The lieutenant slowly focused on him. "I'm through, Mr. Thorgard. Your four days are up. We've a lot of proper burying to do and then I'm going back and send in my report," he said. "I don't think headquarters expected anything like this when they assigned my troop to you."

"Only Mr. Thorgard expected," Fargo snapped, throwing an icy glare at the man.

Thorgard ignored him, his eyes on Tibbet. "You'll take us to Dead Horse Point. You can do your buryin' tomorrow," he said. "Let's move."

Fargo watched the lieutenant slowly consider the demand. "All right. I'll finish the assignment. You've another few hours coming to you," he said, and for the first time, Fargo felt a stab of admiration for Lt. Tibbet. He swung the pinto around and moved to the side as the lieutenant started to ride on and the handful of troopers automatically formed a circle around April and the boy.

Fargo's gaze stayed on the boy for a moment; his small face remained virtually expressionless. He'd become as stoic as a Cheyenne warrior, Fargo commented silently, and he fell to the rear of the small band, letting his eyes sweep the hills behind. Nothing moved, and he rode on.

Maybe it was over, he mused. Thunderhawk's actions still didn't fit, not even for vengeance. To save face was important, but not *that* important. An exceptional warrior chief didn't take suicidal action to save face. There was always a balance that had to be kept, and Thunderhawk had a record as an exceptional warrior chief. It still didn't make any damn sense, Fargo frowned. Only now maybe he'd never know anything more. He pushed away further speculation and hurried the pinto forward as the lieutenant picked up the pace.

Twilight had almost slid into night when they reached Dead Horse Point and the sparse collection of shacks took shape. The trading post and the smithy's were the only reasonably sturdy structures, but Fargo spotted one unused shed that seemed in fair-enough shape. He moved alongside Tibbet, reined up, and gestured to the shed. "I'd have everyone bed down in there," he said. "There's room."

"And it's protected," Tibbet said. "It'll do fine for you."

"For us?" Fargo questioned.

"Yes, I've had enough of protecting Mr. Thorgard. My assignment's over, as I said. We'll camp out somewhere. I've a lot of thinking to do. I didn't handle things well at all," the lieutenant said.

"That's a good sign," Fargo answered.

"What is?" Tibbet frowned.

"Knowing when you screwed up. Being able to admit it. A good sign," Fargo repeated.

Tibbet frowned for a moment more. "Maybe," he said. "And maybe it's too late."

"Move out. I don't need you now," Bertram Thorgard interjected.

Fargo half-turned in the saddle to see the knot of horsemen approaching. He stared at them as the lieutenant moved on with the pitifully few remains of his troop. Thorgard spurred his horse forward to meet the new arrivals as they rode to a halt.

Fargo's brow knitted as he counted fifteen men, all of a kind, all wearing sombreros or flat-topped Mexican *poblanos*, all armed to the teeth with at least one pair of pistols and a pair of knives, most sporting thin mustaches on olive-skinned, broad faces. They had two things stamped onto them: Mexican and *bandidos*.

Thorgard greeted the one in the lead, a short-waisted figure with a double row of cartridge belts crossed over his chest, two ivory-handled Model One Smith & Wessons in his gun belt, and two knives stuck into his belt. Small eyes looked out of a slightly puffy face that had small-time arrogance imprinted in its every line.

"Señor Serrano," Thorgard said with welcome in his voice.

"We have been riding around here for two days," the man said coldly.

"There were delays," Thorgard said.

Fargo watched the Mexican's small eyes go to April, take her in the way a fox takes in a particularly attractive young quail.

"My daughter, April," Thorgard introduced her.

The Mexican flashed an oily smile. "And I am Señor Serrano. You may call me Carlos, *señorita*," he said, and made it sound as though he'd bestowed an award on her.

The others looked at April with a combination of interest and contempt. The bandit leader brought his eyes to the Ovaro first, then to the big man atop the horse, his small eyes instantly challenging. "Who are you, *gringo?*" he asked.

"Skye Fargo. They call me the Trailsman," Fargo answered.

The man's face broke into an arrogant grin. "They call me the best and the biggest *bandido* in all New Mexico," he said. "You can call me Señor Bandido." He followed the line with a harsh laugh. "Let's hear it, *gringo*. Let's hear you talk to me with respect."

Fargo eyed the others as they looked on with grins that aped their leader's arrogance. These were really dangerous men. Thorgard had hired more than he bargained for, Fargo grunted inwardly. They were *bandidos*, unquestionably, the worst kind—ruthless, completely amoral, cruel men who would just as soon kill as eat. Some kind of respect had to be established at once, he decided.

"Señor Bandido, go to hell," Fargo said softly, and saw the man's face switch from approval to surprise.

"That was a very *estúpido* thing to say, *hombre*," Serrano hissed.

"No it wasn't," Fargo returned almost mildly. "Because I can outthink, outride, and outshoot any *bandido* I ever met."

"You have the big mouth, Fargo," the man said. "I am going to close it for you."

Fargo saw the man's hand start toward his right holster, and his own hand flew to his side, drew the big Colt in one smooth, split-second motion almost too fast for the eye to follow. He fired twice. The first shot blew Serrano's hat from his head, the second nicked the top of his ear. The *bandido*'s small eyes grew wide in astonishment and he clapped his hand to his ear, drew it away, and stared at the trickle of blood on his fingertips.

"That could've been between your greedy little eyes,

amigo," Fargo said matter-of-factly as he dropped the gun back into its holster.

Serrano looked at him, let his tongue run over his somewhat thick lips. "Very . . . how to say . . . impressive, *hombre.* I will remember this," he said.

"Ard shoot me in the back when the time comes?" Fargo said.

Serrano's oily grin slid across his face. "Exactly," he said. "You see, *hombre,* I am really an honest man."

Thorgard's voice cut in. "I'm sure everything will work out fine," he said soothingly. "Besides, I may not need any of you any longer if Thunderhawk is dead."

The bandit leader gave Thorgard a long glance. "This is possible?" he asked.

"Yes, but I'll pay you in full, just the way we agreed," Thorgard said hastily. "Let's all get some sleep first. We'll bed down in that old shed there," he gestured. "I'll expect your men will stand watch."

"*Sí*, but not where you will see us," Serrano said, and turned an approving glance at April, "*Buenas noches, señorita.*" He grinned. "I hope you will dream of me." He flicked his hand and his men turned with him to ride into the darkness.

"He makes my skin crawl," April breathed.

"You crazy, Thorgard?" Fargo frowned. "What in hell made you hire that crew?"

"I told you, I don't take chances," Thorgard said as he led the way into the shed. "I knew I had the army for only a few days. I had to be ready with somebody else," he said.

"With those rattlesnakes?" Fargo pressed.

"They're exactly what I wanted, men who enjoy killing, the baddest of the bad who have nothing to lose. Moreover, they've all fought the Apache. They're a match for ten Thunderhawks," Thorgard said. "Now let's get some damn sleep and quit jawin'."

"I saw a well outside. I want to wash up," April said.

"I'll go stand watch," Fargo said.

"Serrano's men are on watch," Thorgard growled.

"That's why I'll go with her," Fargo said, and followed April outside as she went to the well with the boy, drew the bucket up, and let the boy wash his face first. Fargo waited to one side as April, when the boy finished, took a kerchief, opened her shirt, and put her back to him. She used her hands to rub the water over herself and the kerchief to dry herself with, but when she buttoned up and turned to him, her skin was still damp and the shirt clung deliciously to each long breast.

"We can go back now," she said.

"He left us alone. Why?" Fargo asked.

"He knows I won't be saying anything now that it's over," April said.

"I've still got questions," Fargo said.

"They're not important now. Neither are the answers," she said.

"Then why can't you talk about it?" Fargo pressed.

"The same reason I didn't have any choice about coming here. Let it go at that, Fargo," she said.

"You said he didn't deserve to always win," Fargo reminded her.

She nodded unhappily. "But he does win," she murmured as she took the boy and hurried past him.

"One thing more," he said, and she paused. "You were going to come visiting."

"You don't know that," she said.

"What if I found another night?" he asked.

"Find it," she slid back, and went into the shed.

Fargo washed at the well and she was under her blanket when he entered the shed, in one corner with the boy. Thorgard lay asleep in the opposite corner and the shed had but one narrow, high window, he noted. Fargo stretched out in front of the door where he'd hear anyone going in or out, and slept almost at once. Maybe answers weren't important anymore. But something still refused to fit right.

The night passed quietly and Fargo was the first to wake inside the shed. By stretching on his toes, he managed to peer out through the narrow, high window. The morning sun had already begun to bake the land, and he could see no one outside. Yet he opened the door carefully before he stepped out. He paused for a moment just outside the door as he scanned the terrain. He saw Serrano's men. They had positioned themselves in a semicircle on the slope of a low hill, far enough away to be out of sight and yet able to see the shed under the moonlight. They were experienced, he muttered grudgingly. And completely untrustworthy. As he saw them begin to gather themselves, he washed at the well and stepped aside as April emerged with the boy. Thorgard was last, and he'd just finished when the knot of riders came along. Serrano's eyes lingered first on April, Fargo noted, then went to Thorgard.

"This Indian of yours, he did not show last night. Maybe you are right. He is dead," the *bandido* leader said, disappointment in his voice.

"That's fine with me. All we have to do then is settle up, my friends," Thorgard said.

April cut in, a tone of hushed awe in her voice. "Not yet," she breathed. "God, not yet."

Fargo followed her gaze to the top of the hill where Serrano's men had been camped. The tall, bronze-skinned, handsome figure sat quietly astride his horse, black-coal eyes burning. Behind him, five more near-naked figures sat on their ponies as if carved in stone. Fargo stared up at the Cheyenne in disbelief and the *bandido* leader's voice cut into his thoughts.

"Those six? They are the ones?" Serrano asked. Thorgard nodded and Serrano flashed his oily smile. "It will be, how you say, the play of children," he commented. "We will get some supplies and be ready to ride in a few minutes." He turned and headed for the trading post, and Fargo's gaze went to the top of the hill again. Thunderhawk raised one arm, clenched his fist, and shook it three times, the sign of undying challenge, the promise of victory.

Fargo turned to Bertram Thorgard and felt anger surging through his powerful body. "Why?" he thundered. "Why is he still after the boy? Don't give me any more saving-face shit. I want the truth."

"He's crazy, that's why." Thorgard said.

"Hell he is," Fargo said, and his angry eyes went to April. "It's past time for holding back, dammit. You said there was no reason to talk because it was over. Well, it's not over. Why, dammit?"

"You keep your mouth shut, girl," Thorgard roared.

April spun on him, the hazel-flecked eyes suddenly flaming with green fire. "No, no more. I've been quiet too long now," she said. "You've hurt too many people. You're a madman. You think you can play God with other people's lives." She whirled from Thorgard and Fargo saw the pain mixed with the anger in her eyes. "Thunderhawk never captured the boy," April threw at him. "There was no boy with the wagon train. He took Mary."

Fargo felt the frown dig into his brow as the thought formed inside him and found words. "And made her one of his wives," he added.

"Yes." April nodded. "The boy is his son."

"Jesus," Fargo breathed. "His son." The words spun inside him, suddenly setting all that had defied logical explanation into place. Bertram Thorgard's heavy face was suddenly drained of color. "You took his son," Fargo said, a new anger surging through him. "A Cheyenne chief's son, goddammit."

"And he doesn't really care about the boy," April cut in. "He doesn't give a damn about the boy being his grandson. The boy is only a way to get back at Mary."

"Don't listen to her," Thorgard suddenly shouted, the veins in his neck bulging.

"It's true," April bit out. "He's mad, obsessed. Mary ran away finally. He had all kinds of people searching for her. But she escaped them all and joined that wagon train. She'd gone, and all his power and money couldn't reach her. He'd organized a posse to go after the train when the attack came." April paused to look at Thorgard, who glared at her with a face still without color. "Only it didn't end there," April said, returned her eyes to Fargo. "Mary struck back at him again."

"How?" Fargo frowned.

"He found someone, an old Pawnee scout. He sent him to Thunderhawk and offered to buy Mary's freedom. He offered Thunderhawk whatever he wanted in exchange for Mary," April said.

"Anything," Thorgard suddenly shouted. "Anything he wanted: jewels, gold, guns, anything."

"But he refused," Fargo said.

Thorgard's lips worked, but it was April who answered once again. "It was Mary who refused. She sent word that she'd rather stay with Thunderhawk than go back with him."

"The bitch," Thorgard exploded, his face contorted with rage. "The goddamn little bitch. She said she'd rather be a stinkin' Cheyenne squaw than come back to me." He strode back and forth, his hands clenched so tightly they lost their color, too. "She died laughing at me, cursing me, making a fool out of me. And after all I'd done for her. Word got around about what she'd done, my own daughter deciding to be a goddamn Cheyenne squaw after I tried to buy her free. Nobody does that to Bertram Thorgard, nobody, and certainly not that little bitch." He paused in his pacing, and his imperiousness flooded back over him. "I couldn't let her get away with it. She was coming back, goddammit. She was coming back."

"In the boy," Fargo said.

"That's right," Thorgard thundered. "In the boy. She was coming back in the boy. There'd be no part of my daughter in a goddamn Cheyenne camp. I'd take the boy. I'd reach into her damn grave and bring her back. Nobody spits in my face and gets away with it." He paused, drew himself up very straight, and glared at Fargo. "I have the boy. I'm going to win, and she'll know it. Somehow, she'll know it."

"You are mad," Fargo said. "You rotten, self-centered bastard. You lied to everyone because you knew nobody'd go along with stealing a Cheyenne chief's son, no matter what you paid them. Because of your damn lies over a hundred men have died."

"That's water under the bridge now. That dammed Indian is as good as dead and I have the boy," Thorgard flung back. "That's all I care about. I've done what I wanted to do."

Fargo glanced up to see Serrano and his men returning from the trading post. "Mount up," he said to April. "We'll talk more later."

She nodded, took the boy, and climbed onto the gray gelding.

"Ready, *amigos?*" Serrano said, and Thorgard nodded. "We go south, into the hills. It will not take long to get rid of this Indian." He turned his horse and his scurvy lot swung after him, all tossing quick, eager glances at April. Fargo fell in behind April as the band made for the hills.

"Keep hold of the boy and stay close to Serrano's men," he said, and she frowned at him. "They're bloodthirsty killers, but they know what they're doing. They know how to fight Indians." She nodded and he brought the pinto up beside her. "Why'd you hold back all this time?" he questioned.

"Aunt Tessie, the woman I've lived with all these years," April reminded him, and he nodded. "He owns the land she's on. He said if I didn't help him he'd throw her off in her wheelchair." Fargo swore silently. Bertram Thorgard's self-centered obsession was rooted in his uncaring ruthlessness. "But suddenly I couldn't go on. I'll stay with Tessie. We'll find a way out, somehow."

Serrano's gesture interrupted them and Fargo swung the Ovaro up along a wide pathway. They were into the Mantila Sal region now, good forest with plenty of rock formations mixed in.

Fargo allowed a grim smile to edge his lips. Serrano was entering terrain made for Thunderhawk. He was letting the Cheyenne think he was stupid. Fargo fell back a half-dozen paces, searching the high land as they rode with his practiced eyes. But it wasn't until midafternoon, when they halted at a stream for water, that the Cheyenne appeared—Thunderhawk atop a small ledge, the others below him, The Cheyenne chief's burning-coal eyes scanned the riders below and Serrano paid no attention to him. Quietly, the bronze-skin figures vanished into the forest cover.

"Soon," Serrano grunted as they set off again.

The day began to close down, gray-purple haze filling the air, and Fargo pointed out a clearing at the foot of a series of rock steps with thick brush and birch. "Good enough, Señor Trailsman," Serrano said, and began to make camp. But eight of his men stayed in the saddle, Fargo noted.

April and the boy settled down to one side when Fargo saw the movement up above him and the two braves came down the slope, riding hard, one at the left of the small camp, the other at the right. Serrano motioned and the eight men on their horses broke into two groups of four each and raced out to meet the Cheyenne before they reached the bottom of the slope.

As Fargo watched, the Cheyenne pulled their ponies to a skidding halt, turned, and began to race away. One flew up the slope, but the other seemed to have trouble with his pony. Serrano's men closed in fast, pulled rifles from saddle cases, and fired. The Indian ducked his horse in between a tall boulder and a thick cluster of birch and glanced back with panic in his face. The four *bandidos* took spurs to their horses and hurtled forward. They were going full speed when the hail of arrows shot from the thick tree cover. Three of the men went down at once. The fourth tried to twist his horse around, but two more arrows caught him through the back of the neck. He fell to the ground on his face, the two arrows sticking up from his neck as though they were giant knitting needles in a bundle of wool yarn.

"*Papanatas!*" Serrano bit out, and kicked at the ground. Fargo swung from the saddle and met the *bandido* leader's angry eyes.

"He just cut the odds by almost a third," Fargo remarked.

"He was lucky," Serrano growled, and waited for the other four *bandidos* to return, their shrugs answering his unasked question.

Night began to slide across the hills and Fargo watched as Serrano gathered his men together and gave instructions in terse, staccato Spanish. Two of the men climbed up onto a rock overlooking the camp. He saw two more disappear into the hills and another two begin to climb upward as night fell.

April moved to where Fargo lowered himself to the ground, the boy in tow. "What's he doing?" she asked.

"Setting up sentries on sentries. The four last ones will lose themselves in the hills, but always where they can see the two on the ledge," Fargo said. "He's figuring Thunderhawk will try to pick off the clearly visible sentries. Then the others will open fire."

"What do you think?" she asked.

"It can work," Fargo said. "The two on the ledge will make a damn attractive target. It'll fail only if the

Cheyenne spot each of the other four, and that's not likely."

April sat back, fished in her pack for some beef jerky, and gave a piece to the boy. He took it in silence and ate with slow, measured bites, as though eating were a duty. The boy's stoicism was not environmental as he'd thought, Fargo realized now. It was in his blood, part of his heritage. He was too young not to be afraid, but he made sure no one saw any signs of it. After all, he was the son of a great warrior chief.

Fargo pulled his eyes from the boy and glanced over to where Thorgard sat with Serrano. *Bastard,* he murmured silently. April put her head back against a tree beside him and he saw the weariness in her beautifully modeled face.

"I'm tired, Fargo," she said. "Tired of all of it, the vengeance and the killing and all the rottenness of it. Mostly I'm tired of his winning. He's going to win again, isn't he?"

Fargo hadn't time to consider an answer when the short, half-strangled sound came from the ledge above. He leapt to his feet, the Colt in his hand, and saw Serrano do the same. He peered up at the ledge. One of the sentries lay dead, a Cheyenne standing over him with a knife in his hand. The other sentry tried to struggle with a second Cheyenne and lost as Fargo saw the hunting knife plunge into his belly. The two Indians spun around to leap from the ledge into the nearby tree cover. They never made it as the shots rang out. Fargo counted six and the two Cheyenne whirled, spun, seemed to do a short war dance before they fell headfirst from the ledge.

"*Bueno,*" Serrano chortled.

"That leaves four," Thorgard exulted, and Fargo met April's eyes.

"It's getting harder for him to lose," Fargo said softly.

"Damn him. Damn his rotten hide," April murmured as she turned away. "I'm going to get some sleep. It's become my hiding place."

Fargo watched as she walked to the side of the camp near Thorgard, tied the boy to her wrist with a leather thong, and lay down in her clothes.

The four *bandidos* returned to camp and settled down as Serrano posted two sentries, one at each end of the small half-circle. He didn't need more, Fargo agreed. Thunderhawk couldn't risk an attack directly on the camp. The site was too tight, its very closeness an effective means of self-protection. He settled himself against a tree, loosened his clothes, and shut his eyes. But he put the Colt on the ground beside his hand before he slept.

The remainder of the night was quiet, and he woke with the sun. He found a bush of wild cherries and munched on them as the others woke. He saw Serrano checking out his guns. "You're almost down to half your men, friend," Fargo remarked.

The *bandido*'s eyes speared back at him. "I can afford six much more than he can afford two," the man said.

"You're right, there," Fargo agreed, turned away, and watched the man out of the corner of his eye as he walked to where April had risen and untied the boy. Tired, angry, her clothes wrinkled, she still managed to look composed. He'd have to find that night, he reminded himself. Before it was too late. If Thunderhawk won, he'd spare no one, Fargo knew.

Serrano called for an early start and rode to a mountain stream, where they washed in small groups while the rest stayed on guard. They rode on through the morning and Fargo noticed that Serrano didn't move too far up into the hill country. He cut across and stayed along wide paths wherever possible, holding to terrain that let him sweep the surrounding land with his gaze instead of being plunged into it.

The sun had gone into the noon sky and burned down hard when they stopped at a small, spring-fed pond. Serrano kept a ring of guards watching the hills as the others watered the horses and filled canteens. He had earned a healthy respect for Thunderhawk despite his surface contempt, Fargo thought, smiling inwardly.

The Trailsman let his own eyes sweep the high land as they rode on and he stayed at the rear behind April.

"You insult me, *amigo,*" Serrano said to him when they paused against to rest. "Do you really think I would shoot you in the back while we are riding along like this?" He smiled.

"Yep," Fargo said cheerfully, and returned the *bandido*'s smile. "The only reason you haven't so far is because you figure you might need every gun you have."

"You misjudge me," Serrano said, laughing, and spurred his horse forward.

"Hell I do," Fargo muttered under his breath. He brought the Ovaro up alongside April as she rode in silence, her fine-edged lips tight.

The sun had started to slide into the late afternoon and the path they were on took a sudden, sharp curve. As they rounded the curve, Serrano reined up sharply and Fargo saw the young tree that had fallen across the path. His gaze flicked to the trunk where it had broken.

"Hit the ground," Fargo yelled, diving from the Ovaro.

Serrano frowned, glanced about for an instant, and dived from his horse. Fargo saw the arrows whistle through the air as he hit the ground, five of them slamming into two of the *bandidos* before they even started to leave the saddle. The long shafts quivered violently in their targets as the two men seemed to fall from their horses in slow motion.

Fargo lay on the ground, the Colt in his hand, and heard Serrano's men firing back furiously. But it was aimless fire, for their attackers had fled into the tree cover on both sides of the pathway.

April sat frozen in the saddle with the boy. Her eyes went to Fargo as he pushed to his feet, accusation in their green depths.

"You were safe," he told her. "He wouldn't risk hitting the boy."

She blinked, let the anger fade from her eyes, and drew a deep breath, and he walked around the horses to where Serrano had just picked himself up. The *bandido* leader's face was grim as he stared at his two dead men.

"That makes you down to seven men, not counting Thorgard and me," Fargo observed. "I'd say he's doing a right good job of whittling."

Serrano only glared and strode past him to stare at the tree. "How did you know, *hombre?*" he asked.

Fargo pointed to the base of the young tree. "It was cut halfway through," he said. "They pushed it to break off the other half."

Serrano's eyes took in the jagged break that went only halfway through the young trunk, and met the cleanly cut other half. "You are good, *hombre,*" he said slowly. "But I am good, too. That *roñoso* will not do it again. I will take him next time." He barked orders at his men and climbed onto his horse.

Fargo returned to the Ovaro and mounted up, his gaze sweeping the forest land on both sides as he rode beside April. Serrano had broken his men into small units, not more than three each, and he kept them riding spread out behind one another.

As the day neared its close, Fargo spied a cleared area a dozen yards into the woods, and Serrano nodded agreement. They made camp quickly, staying in a tight knot. April put her blanket down where Fargo stretched out, the boy tied to her wrist again.

Fargo lay quietly beside her and saw Serrano's men push themselves into the brush on their bellies. They left bedrolls, blankets, and clothes to simulate sleeping figures. It was too old a trick. Thunderhawk wouldn't fall for it, Fargo knew. He'd search the nearby brush and find the figures lying in wait. Fargo's brow furrowed. Serrano would know as much, he pondered. He had to have something else in mind.

Fargo turned on his side, brought the Colt out, and held it in his hand. He was beside April and the boy. The Cheyenne could try to sneak in close enough to take him, Fargo mused. He grimaced and let the camp settle down to stillness as his ears strained to pick up the sounds of the night forest.

He heard nothing unusual, not even the soft tread of mule deer. Except for the buzzing, humming sounds of night insects, the night was still. April had fallen asleep alongside him; she lay on her back, and he enjoyed the slow, rhythmic rise and fall of the long breasts. He let himself catnap, his outer senses asleep, his inner ones alert and tuned to the slightest sound. The night wore on into the deep hours when he caught the faint sound, a sudden rustle, and the darkness exploded in a fusillade of gunfire.

Fargo snapped awake, remaining prone, the Colt raised in his hand. The gunfire had come from the trees at the other side of the camp. He heard the shouts and the sounds of thudding feet as the others sprang awake. "Two of them, Carlos," a voice shouted from the trees, and Fargo rose, helped April to her feet as three of Serrano's men came into sight dragging two slain Cheyenne with them. Two more of the *bandidos* followed and spoke to Serrano. "They got Pablo before we could stop them," one said.

"You didn't watch close enough, idiots," Serrano snapped angrily.

"They were on him before we saw them. They didn't make a sound," the one *bandido* said.

"It's over. I don't want to hear excuses. Get rid of these two," the *bandido* leader growled.

Fargo saw Thorgard standing near Serrano, a grin on his face. "But you got two more. That means there's only him and one more left," the man said. "He's as good as dead."

Serrano spat a contemptuous look at Thorgard. "You have a big mouth, Señor Thorgard. I have lost another man. I am down to six men. *Six*, dammit, and he is still out there. Don't talk to me about him being dead. Not yet," he said, and strode away.

Thorgard shrugged and sat down, satisfaction still on his face. April's hand tugged at Fargo's sleeve and he glanced down at her, seeing the questions in her green eyes.

"I can put it together now," he said. "Serrano set half his men into the brush to lay there and make it seem they were waiting, watching the camp for an attack. But he knew Thunderhawk would spot them as he crept toward the camp. But he'd sent the other half of his men up into the trees with orders to stay there, wait, and watch the ones on the ground. When the Cheyenne went for the *bandidos* they thought were watching the camp, the others poured gunfire down on them. They lost one man, but it worked."

"It's still two against eight, counting you and Father," April said.

"Good odds, but maybe not good enough," Fargo said. "Serrano knows it, too. That's why he's getting nervous." He pulled her to her blanket beside him. "Get some sleep. There'll be nothing more tonight," he said. She lay back and closed her eyes, anxious to hide again in sleep. He did the same a few minutes later. He slept restlessly, though nothing woke him, and felt a strange sourness in his mouth. Forcing himself to lie still, he slept the few hours that were left of the night, and the sourness stayed with him.

8

It was still with him when he woke with the new sun. Nothing he'd eaten, he knew—the sourness came not from the stomach but from the spirit. Fargo pushed himself onto one elbow just in time to see Serrano talking to one of his men who was already mounted and ready to ride. As he watched, the man put his horse into a gallop and raced from the campsite. Fargo rose, threw Serrano a speculative glance, but the *bandido* leader turned away. The others began to stir and wake, and Fargo adjusted the stirrup leather on the pinto as April rose, washed up out of her canteen, and let the boy finish the water.

"We ride slowly today," Serrano said. "And we look carefully every step we take. Let us ride." He turned his horse from the camp onto a path that led east across the hills, avoiding passages that led to higher land again. He led a cautious pace, Fargo saw, almost keeping the horses at a walk, letting his men ride side by side as Fargo stayed alongside April and the boy.

"Another of his men is missing." April frowned.

"He sent him off somewhere," Fargo told her. "I don't know any more than that, except that it wasn't out for a morning canter." He turned his attention from April as Serrano halted, and Fargo saw why. The path narrowed, a thick tree-covered slope on one side, heavy forest land on the other.

"Get your rifles out," Serrano hissed at his men. "Stay alert." He moved his horse forward, a slow walk along the narrowed path, and Fargo's glance took in the slope of the land at the left—steep, but not too steep for an Indian pony. The forest to his right was so thickly wooded he could barely see through the trees.

Serrano kept the careful, slow pace, and he was halfway through the narrowed part of the path when the explosion of brush and leaves erupted from the forestland at the right. Fargo heard the sharp war cry and the thunder of a lone horse's hooves. He glimpsed the horseman racing toward the path through the trees, caught a flash of burning-coal eyes.

"Fire. Shoot. Get him," Serrano screamed, and his men swung rifles around as one, laying down a barrage of gunfire.

Fargo saw the shots send pieces of tree flying, smash through branches, and hit into solid trunks. He also saw Thunderhawk flattened atop his pony swerve once, swerve again, and race away. The arrow that hurled itself through the air came from the other side of the pathway. It hit the *bandido* next to Serrano with such force that it came partially out through the front of his chest. Fargo saw Serrano spin in the saddle as his men pitched faceforward to the ground.

"Over there, get him," Serrano shouted, and Fargo

saw the Cheyenne start to race up the slope as the *bandidos* lost precious seconds bringing their rifles around. He would have been safely away, but Fargo saw the pony slip, lose its footing on something, probably a bed of wet moss. The horse went down on one knee and the Cheyenne fell from its back. That was all the time the riflemen needed. Four shots slammed into him as he tried to climb back onto the pony. Fargo watched him slide to the ground and lie still as the pony raced up the slope.

"You got him, you got him," Thorgard shouted in glee. "He's alone now, nobody left but him. He's finished, goddamn, finished."

Serrano turned his horse forward. "Let's get out of this place," he growled, not even glancing down at his slain man.

Fargo followed beside April, and when the narrowed pathway widened again, he saw a glen of silver firs open up at the foot of a rock formation.

"We stop here," Serrano said, and pulled his horse into the glen.

"Why?" Thorgard asked.

"You'll find out soon enough, *señor,*" Serrano growled. "I have lost still another man. I am down to five men, besides you and that *hombre* who spends all his time with the *señorita.* This will cost you more than we agreed upon."

"Fine, fine, whatever you want. Just finish off that damn Indian," Thorgard said, and Serrano moved away to sit down with his men.

April settled under a shade tree, keeping the boy at her side. Fargo had almost reached her when he saw the lone figure appear on a flat rock above the half-circle of firs. Serrano saw the bronzed figure and leapt to his feet to stare up at the Cheyenne chief. Thunderhawk peered down at them with his burning-coal eyes, sitting motionless on the brown horse. Fargo saw the others nervously lick their lips and clench their fists.

"He's taunting us, damn his red soul," Thorgard blurted.

"He's counting, measuring, taking stock," Fargo said.

"But he can't hope to take the boy back now," April said. "Against all of us?"

"Hope's got nothing to do with it, honey," Fargo said. "Skill, strength, tactics, that's what it's all about." He kept his eyes on Thunderhawk as the Cheyenne continued to sit unmoving. The sound of horses riding hard broke the silence, and Fargo turned, the Colt in his hand at once, to see the five riders appear. One was the horseman Serrano had dispatched at dawn, and Fargo speared the *bandido* leader with a disdainful stare. "Reinforcements?" he said.

"*Sí*," Serrano snapped. "That Indian, he is a bad one. Like Señor Thorgard, I take no chances."

Fargo glanced at the four new arrivals. They were cut from the same cloth, two younger, apprentice killers, Fargo noted silently. His eyes flicked up to the rock, but the lone horseman had vanished.

"He can't expect to have a chance now," April said.

"Maybe," Fargo said.

"He's finished. He just doesn't know it," Thorgard put in, triumph in his voice.

Fargo saw April turn away. "We ride now," Serrano said. "I'll take the boy."

April halted, frowning at the man as he approached. She looked at Thorgard and the man shrugged.

"Señor Serrano knows what he's doing," Thorgard said. "Give him the boy."

April stepped back and the *bandido* leader yanked the boy up by one arm, set him roughly in the saddle, and swung up behind him. He waved one arm forward and the others fell in behind him, the new arrivals drawing up last. April came alongside Fargo as he took the rear again, a disdainful smile on his lips.

"Serrano knows what he's doing, all right," Fargo said. "The boy's going to be his personal insurance. He's realized that no arrow came anywhere near you because the boy was too close."

"He's really quite a coward in spite of all his guns, isn't he?" April said.

"The kind of coward that's dangerous, the kind that uses killing to cloak his cowardice," Fargo said. "He'll kill you, your pa, me, or any of his own men to save himself if he has to."

"What happens now?" April asked.

"That's in Thunderhawk's hands," Fargo answered, and put the pinto into a trot as Serrano increased his pace.

The lone figure appeared twice more before the day ended, always on high, staring down with his burning-coal eyes, vanishing as silently as he appeared.

As night descended, Serrano pulled into a flat area lined on one side by a dozen tall boulders. Using the boulders to form a wall, he made camp and kept the boy with him. He set up sentry shifts to face the three-sided perimeter, and Fargo settled down against the stones at the very tip of the area. As the moon rose, he saw April's willowy form come toward him, her blanket under one arm. She didn't speak until she had settled down, shed her shirt under the blanket, and stayed modestly covered.

"Will he try tonight?" she asked.

"No. This place is too protected," Fargo said.

"But he will try," April said.

"He's come this far. He can't turn away now," Fargo said.

"It's like a terrible play that has to be carried through to the end," she observed soberly.

"That about says it," Fargo agreed.

"Even the ending is already written," April said. "There are too many of them now. But he'll try and they'll kill him and Bertram Thorgard will win once again. Maybe that's the part I hate most."

"Go to sleep," Fargo said gruffly. "Wringing your hands about it won't help any."

"Will anything?" she threw back.

"Maybe. Maybe not," Fargo said as he closed his eyes. But the sourness inside him had taken shape again. It wasn't shame, but it sure as hell wasn't pride. He let it go at that as he fell asleep.

Morning came all too quickly and he woke, rose, and watched as April set up and managed to don her shirt without showing more than a glimpse of bare shoulders. Serrano took the boy with him after they breakfasted on wild plums and drank from a small, clear stream. April brought her horse alongside Fargo's as he swept the land with a long, probing glance. "Do you see him?" she asked.

"No, but he's there, someplace," Fargo said, and swung to the rear of the others as Serrano set out across a small plateau. When noon came, the sun was burning hot and the *bandido* turned upland, rode steadily into the hills where the tall rock formations replaced thick forestland. He drew to a halt where a clear space opened up in the midst of a series of craggy rocks with numerous passageways winding among them.

"We stay here," he said, beckoned to one of his men, and spoke quickly and sharply. The man nodded, dismounted, and took two more of the new arrivals with him. Fargo dismounted, scanned the area, and took in the tall pines that dotted the rocky terrain. The twisted dwarf maples gave an eerie feel to the starkness of the rocks. As April brought the gray beside the Ovaro, he saw the three men return, pulling a broken piece of young maple that had been hacked clean of branches. They took it to the center of the cleared area and drove it into the ground. When they'd finished, Serrano pulled the boy with him to the makeshift stake. He tied the boy to the stake with a dozen rounds of a rawhide strap. Fargo glanced at April as she stepped forward, her brow furrowed.

"What are you doing?" she said, frowning.

"He wants the boy. I'm leaving him out here for him. All he has to do is come take him," Serrano said, ending his words with a hard laugh.

"You can't do that," April protested. "He's a boy. He's not a goat to stake out as bait."

Serrano's face darkened. "Don't cackle at me or I'll put you next to him," he snapped.

April spun on Thorgard. "Can't you stop this? You're paying him," she accused.

"He's doing what I'm paying him to do, finish off that damn Indian," Thorgard said."You mind your own damn business."

April whirled, flung contempt at the man, and strode to where Fargo watched. "The bastards," she murmured. "They've got the upper hand. They don't have to be cruel, too."

"It's a kind of cruelty Thunderhawk will understand," Fargo said."And it won't really make any difference. He has to come for the boy. This might only hurry him some."

"Into making a mistake," April said.

"He'll make no mistakes. He'll do what he has to do, win or lose," Fargo said. "Now, you stay here. I'm going to do some scouting."

"What for?" April frowned, concern in her eyes at once. "I don't want to stay here alone.

"Tell you when the time comes. I'll be back soon," he said reassuringly. Her face remained troubled.

Serrano rose as Fargo mounted the Ovaro, and frowned at him. "Where do you go, *hombre?*" he growled.

"Out picking flowers," Fargo said.

"You running out?" Serrano probed.

"Might." Fargo shrugged.

"Let him go," Thorgard cut in. "We've plenty of men. We don't need him."

"Señor Serrano doesn't want to see me go without a hole in my back." Fargo smiled, his eyes on the *bandido* leader.

Serrano's lips smiled, but his eyes were little pools of hate.

Fargo pulled the pinto's head around and moved sideways out of the clearing until he disappeared down the path. He rode slowly and his eyes went to the high land out of habit. Thunderhawk would be to the north, higher in the hills, formulating his plans. Not that he had many options. He knew Serrano would keep the boy staked out until he shriveled to death under the sun or starved to death. He was prepared to wait however many days it took. Thunderhawk would have to come in, and coming in meant just about certain death.

Fargo's lips pulled back in a grimace of distaste, and he concentrated on searching the low ground where he rode. He'd spotted something as they'd come up the hill and he finally found it again. He moved closer to a small area back from the path. It was a leafy place with a thick bed of star moss, and overhead, a rock outcrop formed a low roof. He turned the Ovaro back and slowly made his way up the high land again. He spied a lone tiger lily growing by the wayside and reached down and plucked it loose. He held it in his hand as he rode into the campsite.

Serrano looked at him, and the man's oily smile appeared at once. "I misjudged you, Fargo," he said.

"That's the second time," Fargo reminded him, and handed the flower to April with a flourish. She accepted it but her eyes told him she wasn't comfortable with the underlying currents that swirled around her. "Relax, honey," he murmured to her as he dismounted.

"All right, but you didn't go out picking flowers," she returned quietly.

Fargo's glance went to the sky where he saw the last of the sun disappear over the high hills. The boy was perspiring, he saw, his arms firmly tied behind him around the stake.

"They haven't given him any water all afternoon," April said. "I'm not going to sit by and watch this any longer." She spun, took her canteen, and marched out to the center of the clearing where the boy watched her approach and was unable to hide the gratefulness in his eyes.

"Leave him alone," Serrano called out, and got to his feet.

"Go to hell," April flung back as she reached the boy.

"Get her away from him," the *bandido* ordered one of his men, and the man quickly rose and started toward April. He'd almost reached her when Fargo drew the big Colt and fired one shot that creased the man's hat brim.

"Aiii," the man shouted as he fell backward, fear on his face as he landed on the ground.

Fargo didn't utter a sound, but his eyes bored into the *bandido* leader.

Serrano's lips twitched for a moment and then he forced himself to shrug nonchalantly. "Maybe it's best this way," he said. "Live bait is always best."

"You're a kind and reasonable man," Fargo commented, and Serrano turned away from him. The other man pushed to his feet and hurried away from April as she held the canteen to the boy's lips and let him drink. It was almost dark when she returned and folded herself down beside Fargo.

"Thanks," she said. "I guess we're not very popular here, not that I give a damn." She sat back against a tall stone and darkness blanketed the sight—but only for a few minutes, for Serrano soon had a fire lighted that threw its glow over the entire clearing.

"I expected he'd do that," Fargo said. "He won't give Thunderhawk any chance to sneak in and get the boy."

"I don't know if I can stand this waiting. My stomach's in knots already," April said.

"You can't do anything about it. Make the best of it," Fargo said gruffly, and fell silent.

He put his head back and the night deepened, the firelight bathing the clearing in its orange glow, the boy and the stake clearly visible. Fargo watched the moon rise, slowly sliding its way across the blue-black sky. He brought his gaze back to the small figure tied to the stake and felt the sourness rise up inside him again. He drew a deep breath, felt April's tenseness beside him as the night drew deeper.

The explosion of sound came with the startling suddenness he had expected. It took a moment to zero in on the crashing thunder of hoofbeats and he saw the others leaping up, equally uncertain. The horses burst from a passage to his right, heads tethered together by a rope halter. They raced toward the center of the clearing and Fargo heard Serrano's shouts over the hoofbeats. "He's in between them. Get him from behind," the *bandido* roared.

Fargo saw the *bandido*'s men race out into the clearing, try to circle behind the galloping horses. They fired wildly, trying to aim between the horses.

"He's not there," Fargo heard one figure shout. "There's nobody between the horses."

Fargo spun, peered past the stake, and saw the figure racing from the other side, a hunting knife glistening in one hand. But Serrano had his own catlike reactions as he whirled, quickly aware that he'd been fooled. He saw Thunderhawk and fired, too fast, wild shots, and the Indian dived, rolling to one side. He was only a few feet from the boy, but the others had turned now. Rifle shots plowed into the ground and Fargo saw Thunderhawk roll, leap, dive to one side, and roll again. The shots came close, but the *bandidos* were too excited to take time to aim. The Cheyenne reached the rocks as a bullet grazed his shoulder, but he disappeared through a crevice and was gone.

"Damn," Fargo heard Thorgard swear as he stepped forward. "We almost had him. Next time for sure."

Fargo felt April's hands wrapped around his arm. He met the question in her eyes "Probably," he said. "His luck's bound to run out." He stepped back into the shadows by the rocks and pulled her down beside him. "There'll be no more tonight," he said. "He'll have to take time, plan again, prepare."

She nodded, stayed silent, and he let the camp settle down again. Serrano posted two sentries nonetheless, and Fargo waited until the moon began to slide down the sky. He rose, pulled April up gently, and she followed, her eyes questioning. He took the pinto by the reins and led the horse along the edge of the rocks and down the passageway. He stayed afoot till he was a hundred yards from the camp and then swung onto the horse, April coming up to sit against him.

"Where are we going?" she asked.

"I said I'd find a night and a time," he told her.

"Is this what you went out for this afternoon?" she said.

"Not exactly. I looked for a place we could get to when it finally ended, someplace close and out of the way. I figure Serrano's going to try to finish more than Thunderhawk," he said as he reached the little hidden away place and turned into the narrow opening. "But there's no reason why it can't be used for something else," he said, and slid from the saddle.

"No reason at all," April murmured as he lifted her to the ground. She stayed in his arms, the green eyes suddenly imploring. "Make me forget all of it, Fargo," she said. "Just for a while."

Her lips reached up to his and he brought his hands up to press against the sides of the long breasts and he felt their softness through the shirt. Moonlight filtered little shafts of silver through the foliage, slanting in under the rock outcrop. April unbuttoned the shirt, let it fall from her shoulders. The long breasts were beautifully curved, a slow smooth line that came to the full bottoms where tiny pink points stood firm on equally small pink circles. He cupped the full cups in his hands; she shuddered, and he saw her tongue come out, rest on her lips, snake forward, and taste the air.

She yanked the skirt free, pushed down, and stepped out of bloomers and let him see the tall, willowy body that curved with the slender grace of a marsh cattail. A small waist flowed into narrow hips and a flat abdomen with a tiny indentation. Her thighs were slender stalks that avoided being sticklike with the flowing line of youth. Below her flat belly, a V of twisting, curly tendrils reached out and fell against the whiteness of her legs.

"Come to me, Fargo," April breathed. "Come to me." Her hands reached out, helped him shed clothes, and when he stood naked before her, he knew he was already erect, his maleness reaching with hunger. She gazed at him, gave a small gasp of awe and delight, and sank down on the soft, cool moss. She cupped one hand under her left breast and pushed it up to his lips—an offering, the chalice of the flesh given up to be taken. He closed his lips around the full cup, felt the tiny pink tip hard and erect in his mouth.

He drew slowly on the long breast, sucked, caressed,

savored. "Yes, oh my God, my God, yes," April murmured and her hands pushed through his hair, pressed his head harder down onto the breast. "Aaaah . . . aiiii . . . oh, God, yes," she gasped out as he caressed the nipple with his tongue, pulled gently on it with the edge of his teeth, and heard her small cry of delight. His hand moved down the willowy body, explored its curves and hollows, slid across the flat belly, and pressed down on the twirly, tangled triangle.

His hand moved down, and her slender thighs fell open as the petals of a sunflower fall open. He touched the sweet dark place and she half-screamed in pleasure. Her skin was damp. She was warm and wet and waiting, and he felt her hand come down to find him and close around him as she cried out in satisfaction. He let her guide him gently, heard her quick gasps of delight as she held him, brought the shaft to the throbbing, flowing entranceway.

"In, in, God, come in me, Fargo," April cried out with sudden vehemence. Her hips rose and thrust upward as though all waiting, all discipline had shattered. He slid forward, into the softness of her, the path made smooth and moist, and she cried out in delight. She let him go in deep, pushed forward to meet his slow thrusting, her fingers digging into his back. He felt the long, slender legs rise up and clasp around his hips as he thrust hard suddenly, thrust again, and she cried out in joy. The long, willowy body began to undulate, her hips lifting, moving from side to side, lifting and pushing against him, moving into the side-to-side motion again. The sensation flowed through him as he felt her tighten, loosen, tighten against him inside her. His own groan of pleasure mingled with her long, soft wails.

"More, more," April breathed, and the willowy body shuddered, moved harder, fiercer with him. "So wonderful, oh, so wonderful," she murmured, and the willowy legs rubbed against him and he felt the curly tangle brush his abdomen as she thrust upward. She made love to him with all her being—body, spirit, all the desires of the flesh let loose. He moved inside her with increasing speed, felt his own body taking control, refusing to heed the orders of the mind. He abandoned control, responded to the wild hungering that was part of her, matched the willowy body's undulating motions, and suddenly he felt her hands tighten against him, fingers dig into his shoulders. April's long neck arched back, and her mouth fell open as if to scream, but the sound was a long, hissing gasp, ecstasy too intense to give voice. He pumped feverishly and felt his own explosion come together with her quivering ecstasy.

"Oh, oh . . . oooooh, yes, oh, my God yes," April breathed as the blinding moment encompassed her, held them both in its fervid grip, and the world was made of pure pleasure and there was nothing more than the flesh and the spirit and he cried out with her in a last agonizing appeal for more. But there was never more, and the ecstasy became only wonderful warmth. He fell onto the soft cool moss with her as she breathed in quick, gasping sounds.

He stayed in her until his own burning embers faded away, and he finally rolled onto his back, bringing her face against his chest. He gazed at the lovely willowy body that curled languorously half over his groin. The green eyes met his gaze and he caught the flash of smugness in them.

"Wild enough for you?" she murmured.

"Wild enough," he said, and laughed at the unsaid in the question. She lay with him, the long breasts beautifully soft against his chest. He saw the faint first light of dawn through the thick leaves and pushed onto his elbows."Good morning," he said, kissed her, and felt her lips answer at once.

"What if we just keep riding?" she said. "Not go back at all."

"Why not?" he asked.

"I don't want to go back," she said. "Will they come after us?"

"No, they can't afford to do that," he said.

"Then let's go on, run," April said, and lifted herself to sit up, the long breasts swaying beautifully as she grew excited.

"We're going back," he said quietly.

"Do you have to see how it ends?" she accused. "Do you have to be in at the kill?" He saw the anger flare in the hazel-flecked eyes.

"This time," he said.

"Then you're no better than the rest," she flung at him. "And I thought you were different."

"I've my reasons," he said.

"Tell me," she demanded.

"When it's time," he answered. She glared at him and was uncertain at the same time. "But we don't have to go back till later," he said mildly.

She regarded him suspiciously, but the green eyes suddenly softened and she came forward, her arms circling his neck. "You'd best have a good reason," she said.

"For going back or staying?" he asked.

"Both," she said.

"I'll give you the second one now," he said, and pulled the long breasts up to his mouth.

She made a happy sound and came to him at once. As the morning sun sent its yellow rays through the thick leaves, he made love to her again and she cried out and let her screams greet the new day with the ecstasy of hope and pleasure and renewal.

9

The sun was in the afternoon sky when they returned to the mountain clearing, and Fargo saw April's eyes go to the boy at once. The heat had taken its toll; his small face was strained. Fargo met Serrano's eyes first. The man licked his lips almost in anticipation. "I thought you had taken the woman and run," he said.

"I never miss the last act," Fargo said.

"Good," Serrano said. "We have much to settle."

Thorgard strode over to where April slid to the ground beside the Ovaro. "Bitch," he said. "Not that I give a damn what you do. I've won, that's all that counts. You can't run away from that. You can't and she can't." He spun on his heel and stalked away.

April lowered herself to the ground and Fargo saw the anger and pain in her face as he sat down beside her. He said nothing and let the afternoon slide into dusk. Serrano had the fire lighted again and the clearing stayed bright as night came to surround the rest of the hills. Thorgard sat with Serrano and Fargo saw the eager anticipation burn in the man's eyes.

"He'll try again soon, won't he?" April said softly.

"Not soon," Fargo said. "I'd guess he'll wait till it's almost dawn. The edge will be off their alertness by then. He'll try to work every little thing he can. He has no choice."

"Why did we come back?" she asked. "You said you'd give me the reasons."

"Later," he said. "Get some shut-eye. Nap a spell." He closed his eyes and shut off further questions. He let himself catnap as the night drew on, and when the moon began to near the distant mountain peaks, he gently shook the slender form beside him. She opened her eyes at once, blinking at him. "Time for reasons," he said softly, and she sat up at attention. "We'll start with your own words," he said.

"My words?" She frowned.

"Bertram Thorgard doesn't deserve to win," he repeated. "He's chasing a mad obsession. He has no goddamn business having the boy. Thunderhawk has wiped out all those drifters sent against him. He followed them down to get his son back and finished the last of them. He took on a U.S. Cavalry troop, made them fight his way, to get his son back. He's cut these stinkin' hired killers to ribbons to get his son back. Now he's going to put his life on the line once more to get his son back." Fargo paused, his lake-blue eyes suddenly hard as he met April's gaze. "He deserves to get his son back," Fargo said.

"Yes," April breathed. "But how? What can we do?"

"Give him the boy," Fargo said. "Give him his son." Fargo pushed himself to his feet, pulled April up with him. "You stay here till I call you," he said. She nodded, her lips parted anxiously. He kissed her quickly, "For luck," he said, grinning, and slowly strolled across the clearing. He passed close to the boy and saw the weariness in the small face.

Serrano rose as he came closer, frowned in curiosity. "Go back with the woman," the *bandido* said. "I don't want anyone walking around now. What's the matter with you?"

"Got a question," Fargo said.

"Later," Serrano hissed.

"Now," Fargo said, and suddenly the Colt was in his hand, the barrel pressed against the *bandido*'s temple. "How do you think it feels to have your brains blown out, *amigo?*" he asked. "Good question, no?" He stepped behind Serrano, yanked the man's guns from his holsters, did the same with his knives, and circled one powerful arm around the *bandido*'s neck. Fargo saw the others rise and look on, confusion and uncertainty on their faces. They drew guns, started forward. "They make one move and you'll get the answer to that question," Fargo said as he pressed the barrel of the gun into Serrano's temple.

"Stay back," Serrano ordered, fear in his voice. "This one is crazy," he said in Spanish.

"That's right," Fargo agreed as he backed toward the stake with his captive. He saw the others watching, their guns half-lowered. One man started forward, brought a rifle up, and Fargo pulled the hammer back on the Colt.

"No," Serrano yelled. "Put the damn gun down."

The man lowered the rifle and stepped back.

Fargo neared the stake and called out to April. She came running as he halted, Serrano held in front of him. "Untie the boy," he said, and she knelt down and began to take the rawhide bonds from the small wrists.

"No," the cry came, a strangled sound, and Fargo saw Bertram Thorgard rush forward. "You can't do that. No, no, damn you." Fargo whistled and the Ovaro came toward him at a trot as April untied the last thong. "You won't do this to me. You're not cheating me out of this," Thorgard roared, came forward, and drew the gun from its holster. "I'll kill you, first, damn you," the man shouted, his heavy face twitching.

"No, you old fool, no," Serrano screamed, tried to twist away, but Fargo's grip was viselike.

Thorgard raised the gun, fired, and Fargo spun the *bandido* in front of him. He felt the man's body shudder as the bullet slammed into his chest, and he heard the swift, hoarse explosion of breath. Fargo lowered the Colt as Thorgard fired again, hit Serrano with another slug. The Colt barked and Thorgard clutched at his knee as it shattered and he pitched foward, the gun falling from his hand.

Fargo let Serrano's lifeless body slide from his grasp, scooped up the boy, and leapt onto the Ovaro. The others stared at Serrano's crumpled form, and Fargo sent the Ovaro racing from the clearing as the first gray light of dawn stretched its fingers across the sky. He slowed as he moved up into the rocky higher land, the boy in the saddle in front of him.

The dawn came quickly as he slowed the Ovaro to a walk and picked his way through narrow passages lined with twisted dwarf maples. The horseman was suddenly in front of him, blocking the path, the arrow in place, the bowstring drawn taut.

Fargo halted, his gaze going past the drawn bow

and the arrow aimed at him to meet the burning-coal eyes. Slowly he lifted the boy from the saddle and lowered him to the ground. He watched little legs churn furiously as they raced to the brown horse a dozen feet away.

Thunderhawk slowly lowered the bow, reached down, and scooped the boy from the ground and put him on the horse in front of him.

Fargo spoke in Siouan. "He is your son. I did not know," he said.

The Cheyenne nodded, but the burning eyes did not soften. Slowly he turned the horse and rode into a side passage to disappear from sight.

Fargo drew a deep sigh from the pit of his stomach, wheeled the pinto in a tight circle, and headed back to the clearing. The sun had come up as he rode in, the Colt in his hand. The *bandidos* were gathered together at one end and they'd lain Serrano over his horse. There was no fight left in any of them. They were clearing out.

Thorgard sat on a rock with a shirt wrapped around his shattered knee. April stood nearby. Fargo nodded at the question in her eyes, and she smiled, a slow, wide smile. He halted in front of Thorgard and met the man's baleful stare.

"You lose," he said. "All the way."

Thorgard's lips worked but no words came, and behind the baleful stare Fargo saw the realization of defeat. He glanced at April and she hurried away for a moment, then returned on the gray gelding.

"Let's go back slowly," she said.

"Just what I had in mind." Fargo smiled.

She rode beside him out of the clearing, and when

they reached an open space that let him see high into the hills, Fargo paused. The lone horseman was outlined against the morning sun for only a moment and then he vanished.

LOOKING FORWARD

The following is the opening section from the next novel in the exciting *Trailsman* series from Signet:

THE TRAILSMAN #60: THE WAYWARD LASSIE

1861 . . . St. Louis, Missouri . . .
End of one trail,
beginning of another.

Fargo came groaning out of deep, deep sleep. He was so thoroughly disoriented that he wasn't even aware of it.

His tongue felt like it had grown scales during the night, and his throat seemed coated with a green, nauseous slime. His eyes were glued closed. He forced them open, slowly, one at a time, and discovered dark-brown hair on the pillow next to him. He could remember nothing about the previous night, but he sure as hell must have had a good time. Must have.

Good time or no, though, the loss of an entire evening was worrisome. He simply wasn't the kind of glad-handing hale fellow who went out and got himself wiped-out drunk. He didn't permit himself that sort of thing.

Except this time.

He groaned aloud and rolled onto his back. It was a mistake. The movement—slight though it had been—set off a pounding inside his head that would have done credit to a bass drum on the Fourth of July. Son of a bitch.

The movement also roused the woman who was sleeping beside him. She stirred and rubbed at her eyes, whimpering a little as she came out of her sleep, then turned her head. Her eyes—light brown flecked with gold, he saw now—sparkled into a smile that didn't reach her lips.

"Good morning, Skye." She sounded pleased. Perhaps even a bit smug. My, but he did wish he could remember the night's events.

Fargo blinked, yawned, took another look at her. She wasn't bad-looking. Nice-enough features, except for a small scar at the corner of her mouth. The imperfection was certain not enough to worry about.

She sat up, the sheet that covered the two of them falling to her waist as she raised her arms to fluff her hair. It was a deceptively casual but thoroughly contrived action that all women know shows off their breasts to best advantage. She had much to show off. More than a mouthful, and therefore something of a waste. But such a lovely waste. Her breasts were large, firm for their size, and pink-tipped. In spite of the drumbeat inside his head and the vile taste in his mouth, Fargo found himself becoming aroused. Whatever might have happened during the night, it certainly didn't slow him down this morning.

It occurred to him that he had no earthly idea of who this woman was or what her name might be. That was easily covered. "Good morning, honey."

She gave him a huge smile and a squeal of pleasure when she saw the sheet over his waist begin to rise into a tentlike form.

"You need a hair of the dog, Skye. But nothing serious, hmm? Can I get you a beer? Then we can snuggle back into bed for a little while. Hmm? We don't have to get up so early, do we?"

"That sounds . . . sounds fine." His damned tongue was not only scaly, it refused to function properly.

"Be right back, Skye." She bent down to give him a brief but highly promising kiss on the mouth—Lordy, he wouldn't have been able to stand the thought of kissing a foul thing like his mouth was this morning; his breath surely must be bad enough to gag a goat—and slipped out of the bed. The rest of her body wasn't bad either. Her ass was nicely rounded if a bit flabby. She had a pimple on her left cheek. But Skye Fargo could easily appreciate her overall beauty.

She paused at the door to blow him another kiss, pulled on a light robe, and went into the hallway.

In addition to having no idea of who his sleeping companion was, Fargo couldn't remember where in the hell he was. The fact that she'd gone out in that skimpy robe hinted that they were not in a hotel. A whorehouse? Private home? He just didn't know.

About all he knew—and he wouldn't claim to be

100 percent positive about that either—was that he was in St. Louis. He'd been paid off here, assuming he really was still in St. Louis and hadn't somehow misplaced a thousand miles or so of countryside, after escorting a small but valuable cargo of gemstones from Santa Fe east to the queen city of the West. And now, by damn, he had a hefty poke in his jeans pocket. Enough money that he could take some time for himself and do some serious searching for those sons of bitches who . . . He shook his head impatiently. No point in thinking about that right now. It just got him upset, thinking about the quest that drove him after the men he so desperately wanted—needed—to find and to kill.

He heard footsteps in the hall. The door opened, and the woman was back. She carried a small tin bucket in one hand and a pair of tin mugs in the other. She smiled at him again.

"That didn't take long."

"Of course not."

Still no clues about where they were. Or who she was. He wished he could remember more. More? Hell, he wished he could remember anything.

The woman set the mugs on a bureau and poured foamy beer into them, handing the first to Fargo and taking a smaller portion for herself. "This will make you feel better, Skye."

It did. The sharp flavor cut through the fur on his teeth, washed most of the slime out of his throat, and even seemed to make some of the pounding in his head go away. Some, not all. He still felt like a sack of soggy shit. He was almost used to it, though.

The woman looked at him and smiled, barely tasting her drink. She set her mug aside and took his from his hand to put it out of the way also. With a broad smile she let the robe fall off her shoulders, and she slid under the sheet beside him.

Her mouth covered his hungrily, and her hand searched for him, impatiently shoving the sheet aside and groping until she found him.

Fargo responded with an animal intensity. He moved, taking her right nipple in his mouth and kneading it with a sudden hunger. Again, harder this time, and the woman's mouth opened in a breathless moan of pleasure.

She clutched at him, grasping him, running her hand up and down the length of him, cupping his balls and applying pressure that stopped just short of becoming pain. Her breath was coming quicker. And so was his.

"You're special, Skye. So special." She lay flat on the bed, pulling him over her, and he moved from her breast, down across the soft mound of her belly to tangle in the curling patch of hair at her crotch.

She groaned and parted her thighs, opening herself to his touch. He dipped a finger into her to moisten the tip, then sought and rubbed the tiny button of woman-pleasure that was hidden in the pink folds of flesh there. He rubbed it slowly, in small circles, and she responded within moments, raising her hips to meet his touch, moaning and sighing, her own arousal evident with the quickening tempo of her responses until with a sharp, unexpected cry she clenched her legs tight together and stiffened in a spasm of raw pleasure.

Skye Fargo kissed her gently, allowing her time to come down from the heights she had just reached.

Within seconds she was responding to the kiss, wrapping her arms around him and guiding him over her eager body, guiding him inside.

The heat of her surrounded and enveloped him, and he plunged deep into her. She kept her hand between their bodies, moving it lower to cup its heat around his balls even when he was inside her. The combined sensations of palm and woman flesh worked together to bring him to a fast, thunderous climax.

He groaned out loud as the spurting jets of hot fluid poured from his body deep into hers, and she held him all the tighter as he stiffened and shuddered and expended himself totally into her.

When he was done, he collapsed, dropping his weight onto her sweaty, willing body, and she wrapped both arms tight around him with a sigh of contentment. She seemed every bit as satisfied as he felt himself at the moment. It was quite a step up after the way he'd felt when he woke.

"Mmmm." He rooted for a moment in the hollow of her throat, relaxing, then rolled away from her.

"Can I get you anything else, Skye?"

"After that? I can't think of anything that would top it. But if you can, honey, I'm willing to listen to suggestions."

She laughed and sat up on the side of the bed to get the beers she had poured earlier. She handed Fargo his, and he took another satisfying swallow. Damn, but he wished he could remember more about her. She was something special. Certainly not a bad treat to wake up to on a bleary morning.

If it was still morning. The sunshine beyond her curtained window was strong enough to suggest that he might already have missed the morning and be working on the afternoon hours now.

There was quite a bit he wished he could remember.

He stood, wobbling only a little from the aftereffects of the night before, and reached for his clothes, dropped in an untidy pile on his side of the bed.

"You aren't leaving, are you, Skye?" She sounded disappointed.

"Got to." He had plans. Plans that did not involve the soft living of St. Louis. Pleasant living, true, but not what he had in mind for the next few months. He had more than enough money now to finance the search for the men who had turned him from a normal young man into the avenger he had become.

"You'll see me again?"

"Sure, honey."

"You won't forget?"

"Forget you? Impossible." He finished buttoning his shirt and leaned down to give her a reassuring kiss. Damn but he wished he knew who she was. He really might want to pay her another visit if he had time before he left.

He buckled his gun belt into place, automatically checking the army model Colt .44 to see that it was in good shape and that the brassy gleam of fresh caps showed on the steel nipples. The Sharps carbine leaned against the wall in a corner beside the door.

Best of all was the comforting weight of the gold pulling at his trousers and making a large lump in his pocket. Whoever the woman was, she was no sneak thief. Good. He needed that money to carry him on his search. His efforts on behalf of another man had paid off handsomely enough that Skye Fargo, the Trailsman, could conduct some business of his own.

"I'll see you later, honey," he said.

"See that you do, Skye. I miss you already. I want more of that." On those last few words her voice dropped into a husky sultriness and her eyes quite deliberately strayed below his belt buckle.

Fargo smiled and let himself out into the hallway.

The staircase led down into a kitchen, large and commercial, and then out into a saloon, nearly empty at this time of day, whatever that was. A large clock over the bar indicated it was nearly two P.M. Fargo couldn't remember sleeping that late in . . . hell, he couldn't remember *ever* sleeping that late. Period. He must really have had some time last night.

He went out onto the street—he was still in St. Louis—and the strong sunlight hit his eyes like a blow.

The thought of food no longer seemed so repulsive as it would have earlier. There was a café down the street, and he headed for that, feeling his pocket to satisfy himself that he had enough small change to pay for a meal. Although at this hour it probably would be impossible to get a breakfast. He would have to settle for lunch.

He found no small coins so would have to dip into

the gold Señor Martínez had paid him from the Santa Fe trip. No problem.

He pulled out his pouch, opened it, and spilled a pile of lead slugs into his palm.